THE HUSBANDS OF JASIREY

also by Bonnie Arnot
The Devoted of Jasirey

the Husbands of Jasirey
Bonnie Arnot
Book Two
the Destiny of Jasirey
series
Haley's
Athol, Massachusetts

Haley's
488 South Main Street
Athol, MA 01331
marcia2gagliardi@gmail.com • 978.249.9400

Copy edited by Phillis Scott with editorial consultation.

Cover by Elizabeth Lindgren.

International Standard Book Number: 978-1-956055-35-1
Library of Congress Number: pending

for Lenie,
the best one-woman cheering squad a sister could have
and a generous soul

Our anxiety does not come from thinking about the future,
but from wanting to control it.
—Kahlil Gibran

Love has nothing to do with what you are expecting to get
—only with what you are expecting to give, which is everything.
—Katharine Hepburn

Contents

Destiny Begins

Jasirey bounced on her toes as she stood at the end of an unpaved airstrip on the island of the Devoted, the multicultural society that—after a long search and grueling test—had determined that she was the woman destined to lead them in bringing stability to a precarious world. Three of her new husbands—Lee, Liu, and Fael—stood in a semicircle behind her. They waited for her fourth, Ian, who had flown back to Boston to pick up her teenaged sons from her first marriage.

Only a few weeks before, Ian, a member of the Devoted, had brought his fiancée, originally known as Shannon, to the island to be tested as a candidate for Jasirey. She passed the test, and the course of her life changed drastically, a change that would pull her sons along with her.

Jasirey stilled her racing thoughts when she noticed Lee, Liu, and Fael fidgeting. She had been projecting her nervousness onto them.

"Do not fret, beloved," Fael said. "The Imperiat shall sort your sons."

Master Kai, head of the Imperiat, the ruling body in charge of Jasirey's mission, security, and training, had advised her to allow them to inform her sons of the Devoted, her destiny, and her four husbands. Jasirey agreed since she didn't yet understand it all herself.

Ian's private jet soon landed, and when he, Christopher, and Michael disembarked, Jasirey grabbed her sons in a big hug.

Their mother's enthusiastic affection nothing new, they hugged back but blushed as Ian kissed her. They offered the same shy smile as their mother's when Ian introduced Liu, Fael, and Lee as the close friends he'd brought their mom to meet—his pretext for getting her to visit the island.

The adults took the teens to the island's pond with a picnic supper. As planned, friends of the new family—Kharia and Robin, and their two sons, Kirani and Bazir, who were the same ages as Christopher and Michael—met them at the pond. The teens had become acquainted on the internet before Christopher and Michael arrived and quickly bonded over favorite foods and netless water volleyball. Jasirey's sons would stay with Kharia and Robin since the honeymoon cottage for the newlyweds was too small to house more.

Fael, Lee, and Liu had agreed to refrain from husbandly gestures of affection until the Imperiat's talk with Jasirey's sons. After their picnic, the three men left to spend the night at the training center. Jasirey surreptitiously clasped their hands in thanks.

The four teens chattered nonstop as they followed Kharia and Robin home. The next day not a school day, the island boys had promised Jasirey to deliver her sons to her cabin in the morning.

Not at all sorry to have Jasirey to himself, Ian escorted her to the honeymoon cottage and had her dress to her waist before reaching the cabin.

"What if someone comes?" She hastily pressed fingers to his curling lips. "Smart ass."

❧ ❧ ❧

The next day, flushed with excitement, Christopher and Michael arrived at the cabin for breakfast. Kirani and Bazir intended to show them the island's fishing fleet and caves and introduce them to the artisans of ceremonial swords.

"Saltwater crocodiles live here," Michael said, "at the end of a river where mangrove trees grow. Big suckers."

"Their habitat's off limits." Christopher added in reaction to his mother's pained expression.

The boys tried fresh coconut and didn't hate it. Ian brought up the island leaders' wish to talk to them regarding island customs. Neither objected until told they'd meet the Imperiat by themselves.

Their mom reassured them. "I went to a similar meeting. They'll do most of the talking."

The Imperiat had scheduled the meeting for the cooler early morning. The family set out to walk to the Imperiat domicile. On the way, Michael and Christopher noticed people bowing, hands together with fingers curled around each other, and wondered why their mother responded but not Ian. They had, of course, seen other races and cultural clothes on TV but seldom in person, as the small western Massachusetts town where they grew up lacked diversity.

2

The women on the island wore a variety of clothes—saris, headscarves, dresses, or loose shirts and pants the same as many men wore. When they met people clumped together in groups, no one dressed or looked alike. Their mixed interactions gave the boys a weird outsider feeling.

❧ ❧ ❧

Master Kai greeted them in the foyer, bowed to Jasirey, and kissed her cheeks in dismissal. He led the teenagers to the meeting. Hoping to pique the boys' interest, he explained he had earned the title of master for his proficiency in martial arts.

The Imperiat sat on floor cushions in informal groups to prevent overwhelming the teenagers. They served juice along with tea.

"We wished to meet you and introduce ourselves," Master Kai said. "We call our society the Devoted, a people who pledge to serve Jasirey, a woman divinely called to help the world and bear children destined to continue her work."

The boys paid rapt attention.

"We asked your mother to take a test to determine if she is our Jasirey. She is."

Michael's face darkened. "I knew it. I had a dream she was pregnant, but she said she was too old."

The Imperiat murmured. The child possessed his mother's gift of foresight, not that she admitted to anything more than mere intuition. The Imperiat had gotten a glimpse of her abilities during her selection of husbands in the Imperiatu, the test for Jasirey, with Kimika whom she dubbed her white lion, and Mtombe whose destiny she realized lay away from the island of the Devoted.

"I see," Master Kai said. He leaned in confidentially. "I think she still believes that. She did not lie to you."

The boy's bubbling resentment calmed.

"We, however, believe the world shall be blessed through your mother's children."

Christopher said, "Kids she has from now on, right?"

Master Kai smiled kindly. "Each of Jasirey's children shall play a role in the world."

Christopher's eyes went wide. Michael sat back, crossed his arms, and glowered. He very much resembled his mother.

Master Kai saw no reason to restrain his amusement. "We do not dictate your future. We offer our services, guidance, or training whenever you wish." He spread his hands wide. "Or not. We do not interfere in your right to choose."

Michael continued to frown but lowered his arms. "Training?"

Using motivational catchwords, another Imperiat said, "We represent diverse skills ranging from those of warriors to those of musicians and use computers extensively. Even CGI has a place in our work."

The teens' smiles gave the Imperiat hope that the boys had taken a step toward accepting the people—what the Devoted called themselves. Most telling, Christopher and Michael did not question the people's belief that their mother was Jasirey.

One hurdle remained.

"For cultures to accept Jasirey's daughters and sons, the heritage of various races must be reflected in the children. To accomplish that, Jasirey selects multiethnic husbands."

Christopher's brow knit. "You just get one . . . at a time, I mean."

A woman nodded. "Legally in America. Laws differ in other countries. Here, marriage to one person is our tradition, except for Jasirey."

"Throughout time," Master Kai said, "numerous Jasireys have come to us and played important historical roles. Some chose as many as forty-five husbands."

The boys gaped.

"Your mother chose four, the lowest number recorded. You met them."

"Ian's friends," Christopher said. His hunched shoulders lowered slightly.

"Yes. Here they are already married. In America, your mother will legally wed Ian. She loves all four and considers them family."

Michael sat stiffly. "Do they get to tell us what to do?"

An interesting question. Master Kai hedged. "Does Ian?"

Michael shrugged. "Guess not."

"I suspect such things shall be decided as a family. Your welfare seems most important to Jasirey, yes?"

The boys started at the name.

Two intelligent young men, they had much to contemplate. "Have you any questions for us?" Master Kai asked.

The teenagers shook their heads.

"Thank you for talking to us. Should questions arise, speak to us anytime you wish."

Master Kai returned the teenagers to Jasirey and Ian.

Michael stalked straight to his mother. "Are you pregnant?"

She almost laughed—the one unanticipated question—and swished hair from his eyes. He needed an appointment at the barber. "It's too early to tell."

"And all those guys, Ian's friends, are going to be our stepfathers?"

Christopher butted in. "What do we tell friends?"

Michael chewed his nails.

Jasirey drew Michael into a hug. "We'll figure it out together." She put a hand to her eldest son's face. "You okay, Mr. Christopher?"

"Yeah, but you know. It's weird."

"Believe me, I do. I had quite a few things to say in the beginning, myself. Honestly, though, when I met Liu, Fael, and Lee online, I sensed a connection that grew stronger face to face. Now, I can't imagine living without them."

Recognizing the question burning in both boys' minds, Jasirey sighed. "I believe I was supposed to marry your dad and be your mom. I have no simple answers for why it went wrong."

"We talk about it a lot," Christopher said. "Watching you and Ian . . . " He shrugged. ". . . we like how happy you are."

"Lee's wicked big," Michael said. "Don't they get jealous and fight?"

Ian's domain, he immediately stepped in and laid his hands on the teens' shoulders. "The four of us have been friends a long time. We love your mother and haven't the least doubt she loves us. She shows it in everything she says and does. The two of you, are you jealous of each other?"

"No," they both agreed without hesitation.

Jasirey, Ian, and the teens stopped at the training center to watch Liu, Fael, and Lee spar. The boys had only seen video and movie characters react with their swift precision.

"We practice most mornings to hone our skills and for exercise," Ian said. "If it interests you, we can begin lessons here and continue back home."

Christopher's eyes brightened. "Can we, Mom?"

"You have to realize those moves require years of practice," Jasirey said.

"We practiced at least several times a week," Ian said, "when we prepared for missions." The other men joined them and cut off the teens' eager questions. "We'll tell you stories," Ian continued as he winked at Lee. "Let the big guy here explain landing face down in the mud."

Liu and Fael laughed.

Michael peered up to check if the comment annoyed Lee, who glanced at his feet in embarrassment. Michael's grin reflected his mother's mischievous light as he asked, "You tripped on your own feet?"

Lee's mouth opened. "How did you—"

"He is like his mother." Fael clapped the boy's shoulder.

Michael better understood his mother being drawn to the guys.

"And in what way is Christopher similar to his mother?" Liu asked.

Passing a hand over the teen's springy hair, Ian said, "Quiet except for his guitar playing, intelligent, and curious."

Christopher squirmed, a grin pulling at his mouth.

While helping to make lunch at the cabin, the boys watched fingertips glide over their mother's cheek, quick kisses on her neck, and her affectionate responses.

Jasirey asked them to help set the coffee table in the sitting area. The kitchenette island was inadequate for seating the entire family. "You guys all right?" she asked the boys.

"They like you a lot," Christopher said.

"I like them, too. Doesn't mean I don't feel bad your dad and I failed. How is he?"

"He doesn't seem sad." Michael picked at his cuticles. "He's all excited about his car."

Jasirey had given her ex, Roger, the down payment to replace his high-mileage car, the money for it taken from an account Ian had insisted on setting up for her.

Feeling the weight of his mother's patient waiting, Christopher murmured, "He keeps talking about some woman at work."

"Good. I want him to be happy."

Christopher glanced at his brother. "But what happens if it doesn't work out for him or . . . you?"

"Every relationship has problems," Jasirey said. "I won't speak for your father. For myself, I'm older, wiser, and your stepdads and I have communicated better from the start."

Michael's eyes glinted. "Yeah, they don't let you boss them around."

"Quiet, you." She playfully shook his shoulders, barely able to make him wobble anymore.

"Seriously, the times we've disagreed or gotten frustrated and I withdrew, these guys persisted," she told her sons. "We continued talking, a major area where your dad and I dropped the ball."

"Do we tell Dad about four husbands . . . and everything?" Christopher asked.

"He's aware I'm marrying Ian. Mention the others as Ian's friends. That will probably end the conversation."

Christopher reddened. "Don't think that'll work on our friends. Kind of hard to explain all the touching and kissing."

Michael rolled his eyes.

❧ ❧ ❧

That evening, Jasirey initiated their first family prayers. The boys didn't mind, since no one insisted they say anything and the adults kept it short. Still adjusting to the time difference, the teens were glad when Kirani and Bazir arrived to escort them to their house. Jasirey kissed her sons goodnight and passed them to the men for hugs. Not ready to hug back, the boys tolerated the attention with shy smiles.

Lee swung Jasirey into his arms and settled on the sofa to nibble on her neck. "They're fantastic boys. You're remarkably in tune with them, answering questions before even asked."

Liu sat beside them. "They seem to be adjusting well. Do you agree?"

"They're okay, here anyway. We need a story to explain your presence at home."

"Tomorrow," Lee said. "You're tired." He cupped her breast, frowning as she flinched. "Did I hurt you, little one?"

Jasirey caressed his face. "No, teddy bear. They get tender near my period." Liu rubbed her tummy. She saw him reach for her stomach but, not in the mood for her men's occasional irritation at her body image issues, didn't bat an eye.

"Your abdomen is slightly distended."

She shrugged as she assumed bloating. Liu pulled her legs onto his lap to massage her feet. Jasirey felt her eyelids droop.

"Prepare for bed, precious one. I shall continue the massage on the bed."

After the bathroom door closed, the others turned expectantly to Liu.

"Let us allow her a few days with her sons before I examine her."

❊ ❊ ❊

In the morning, Ian told Jasirey that, while in the States, he had scouted for rental properties to house the Devoted who worked on their stateside home and compound walls surrounding it. Even before coming to the island, when Jasirey was Ian's fiancé, the couple had made plans to build a home in the small town where she and her sons lived.

"Security people," she said, "housekeepers, and groundskeepers will be long-term. Why not build a dormitory outside the compound so they can entertain friends?"

"I'll take care of it," Lee said. "They'll appreciate your thoughtfulness."

He did not inform her that the Devoted tended not to form close outside relationships. Jasirey had to interact in the world. As head of her security with Fael, it gave Lee an uncomfortable insight into the security problems her inclusive calling might engender. Lee noted Fael's concerned look and knew they were on the same page.

"Do you want a place set aside for training?" Jasirey asked the men.

They agreed and planned a two-room building on the grounds within the compound walls, one room as an infirmary for Liu, a healer, to use for his practice.

"Shall we continue family prayers in America?" Liu asked.

"I'd like to. You, Ian, and Fael described your beliefs to me. Teddy Bear, you said you're Jewish?"

"Our German ancestors were Jewish," Lee said. "After World War I, control of Samoa passed from Germany to New Zealand. We

8

became independent about forty years later. Jewish spouses became less common. We intermarried with Christians and combined beliefs—the Sabbath with the Christian Sunday and Passover with Easter. I practice the Ten Commandments and the precept to treat others as you'd have them treat you.

"Buddha also taught it, saying, 'Respect the self of your fellow man as your own self.' In my time here, I have also come to believe in reincarnation. I don't find it incompatible."

Jasirey's gleeful imp challenged. "I love a debate."

Bee to a flower, Lee stepped toward their wife.

Fael interrupted. "I assume dinner is to be family time." She nodded. "Since we will already be together, prayer afterward seems logical."

"Nothing prolonged or formal," Lee said. "We don't want to bore the children. Just concerns anyone has, prayers of thanks—in that vein."

Sounded good to Jasirey. She announced her plans for the second half of their morning by pouncing on Lee.

❋ ❋ ❋

After school, Jasirey and her husbands spent the rest of the afternoon with Christopher and Michael at the pond. Lee's parents, Paul and Alva, had invited the adults to dinner with other friends who shared a love for woodworking.

One older couple had recently finished their probationary period as recruits for the Devoted. Mashita taught the group some fine carving techniques. They knew little about his wife, Satoko.

Not a woodworker, Jasirey watched the others. The Japanese couple sitting slightly apart from the group drew her attention. The woman muttered derisive comments. Her embarrassed husband shushed her until they ended up sniping at each other.

Jasirey inched closer.

Satoko flinched when she looked up to see Jasirey beside her and refused to meet their lady's gaze.

Something burdened the older woman. Jasirey reached for her hand. Satoko's face crumpled, and searing pain flooded Jasirey. She fought the adrenaline-fueled instinct to retreat.

Fael's sudden tension called the other husbands' attention to their wife's distress.

Jasirey drew a steadying breath as she asked Satoko, "What's wrong?" She registered that the room went quiet but continued to focus on the woman's suffering.

Gazing at Jasirey, whose eyes mirrored her pain, Satoko gave not a single thought to refusing their lady. Satoko wordlessly beseeched her husband. Together, they told Jasirey of their life in Japan, he a carpenter, she a caretaker of children. They had a boy and girl who married and bestowed three grandchildren on the doting grandparents. The then-retired couple cared for the young ones while the two sets of parents worked.

They were visiting Mashita's sister inland the day a tsunami carried off everything—their children, grandchildren, and many Satoko had cared for through the years. A recruiter familiar with Mashita's woodworking skills had offered the grieving pair a new purpose.

Jasirey was blunt. "Do you blame yourselves for not sharing your family's fate?"

"We should have been there," Satoko whispered.

Jasirey rubbed at her heart. "You've found no peace here?"

"We remain unmoored," Mashita said, "my wife more than I. She says she is too old to learn the island's childcare protocol, but I think she believes they do not need her."

Jasirey pressed. "You still have the desire and energy to watch over children?"

"Children are life," Satoko said. "They depend on you. You live for them."

"If . . . when the predicted babies arrive," Jasirey said, "we'll need extra hands. Would you consider coming to America?" Was it right to offer? What if there were no babies?

Satoko's hands fluttered, grabbed Jasirey, and clung.

Jasirey relaxed. It felt right.

"You are wonderfully kind," Satoko said.

"You'll need training on American culture, refreshers on infant care," Jasirey said firmly.

An understanding passed between husband and wife. Mashita said, "We shall both join the training." They bowed low.

"He is good with babies," Satoko said as Mashita's forehead met his wife's.

A surge of warmth from their lady dazzled the couple—not joy but a leap of faith that goodness and purpose still existed.

❧ ❧ ❧

Master Kai joined Jasirey and her family at the pond the next afternoon as they dried off in the sun. Christopher and Michael rough housed in the water with Kirani and Bazir.

"The Imperiat heard of your offer to Satoko and Mashita," Master Kai said.

Jasirey gestured at the larger number of people than usual sitting at a discreet distance, heads together, shooting glances at her. "Seems everyone has."

"Yes. Another fine story for the collection."

Jasirey said nothing. It didn't seem a joking matter to her.

"Your invitation particularly concerns the Imperiat, as we arrange for training and the required paperwork."

Abashed, Jasirey said, "I didn't think of that. Was it inappropriate to ask?"

"Quite the contrary. We wondered if you have training in counseling or therapy. The Imperiat alone had knowledge of the couple's background. Yet you recognized their pain."

Her brow winged up.

Knowing she did not understand why others had not seen the couple's suffering, that her gifts were unique, Master Kai smiled. "You have experienced visions prior to those in the Imperiatu, yes?"

"Runs in my family," she said as if discussing hair color. "No big deal. I can count on one hand the dreams I've had that came true. I don't see anything while awake. I certainly missed this." Her waving hand alluded to finding out she was Jasirey.

Master Kai believed her. "Should a possible portent arise while dreaming or awake, please inform the Imperiat."

Jasirey nibbled at her bottom lip, and frown lines appeared between her eyes.

"What agitates you, dear one?"

She clasped her hands together. "I don't think it's anything." She shook her head. "No, it's nothing."

Master Kai waited silently.

She sighed. "When I'm talking to people, especially if it's an intense conversation about something they need help with or I feel strongly about, I feel . . . "—Jasirey cast about for the proper words—" . . . a bridge form between us." Her shoulders hunched up. "It's stupid."

Master Kai leaned forward to draw her attention. "And what do you do with this bridge?"

Ian rubbed her back. "I'm sure she means she feels a connection—"

Master Kai held up his hand for Ian to cease. "Jasirey?"

"Okay." She patted Ian's leg and squared her shoulders. "But this will sound weird." She drew a deep breath. "I send what the person needs over the bridge—sympathy, strength, calm . . . . " Her narration sped up. " . . . courage to do what's right, especially if it will be hard. Ideas on how to solve problems, even nudges to change poor choices." Guilt suffused her face. "Strong nudges."

"Like noetic science," Liu whispered.

"Baby," Ian said. "Your thoughts can't hurt anyone."

"I hope not, but it feels more concrete than mere thought, as if there is or will be an effect. I try hard to censor myself, but that doesn't always work when I get caught up in people's problems."

Master Kai shook off his fascination. He needed to confer with the rest of the Imperiat.

"Should this be an area you wish to . . . explore," he said carefully, "training might provide insight into what exactly occurs with these bridges." He stood. "For now, concentrate on what must be dealt with in the moment."

Jasirey gave him a small smile. "I know. Sufficient unto the day is the trouble thereof."

On The Way Home

Jasirey had visited the island school before her sons arrived and liked how it was structured. Older classes mentored younger ones. High school kids worked part time alongside adults at jobs that interested them. At a school assembly, the children told her stories from their various cultures or stories based on their most precious lady's legend—the Asian woman who persuaded people to move south before an ice age, a woman from the Middle Ages who introduced several ideas to prolong life. Jasirey had difficulty thinking of their stories as more than myths.

The children in the earlier grades asked Jasirey to tell a story. She recited her sons' childhood favorite complete with facial expressions and soft-to-loud vocal intonations for the little, medium, and great big billy goat brothers attempting to cross a troll's bridge. Adept at weaving a tale, Jasirey had the youngsters jumping and squealing, some slightly behind as interpreters caught up.

As she had hoped, Christopher and Michael liked the school.

They enjoyed mentoring the younger kids and, when meeting them in places outside of school while with their mother, got a kick out of the youngest ones as they blurted out whatever popped into their heads and bobbed at her in jerky imitations of the adult bows Jasirey's sons soon realized were aimed specifically at her.

Older kids hung back but soon copied Kirani and Bazir's casual attitude, more in awe of their lady and the babies to be born than of the kids already belonging to her. They did find Michael and Christopher's lack of knowledge about Jasirey, their own mother, odd.

The people treated the brothers and their unusual family the same as anyone else—well, except for their mother—and that lessened the boys' fears.

Their mom and stepdads discussed the story they would use in America. Close to the truth, they decided to introduce Lee, Liu, and Fael as security experts. The boys understood that multiple husbands opened them to ridicule. Adults, their father included, would be up in arms. It relieved them to have a plan.

A week after her sons' arrival, Jasirey ran from breakfast to be nastily ill. Liu held her and waited for the spasms to subside before assisting her from the bathroom floor. "It is time for a pregnancy test, precious one."

"I'm not late—for me. Can you tell anything this early?"

"The blood test will be accurate, the physical a baseline for future examinations."

Deciding not to hover, which would annoy her, Ian, Lee, and Fael kissed Jasirey goodbye. Liu would escort her to the infirmary.

"I can call for a cart if you lack the energy to walk."

"I'm okay." She gave him a speculative look. "You're carrying a phone? I've never noticed any of the Devoted using cell phones."

Liu removed a landline receiver from a cabinet. "We lead simple lives by preference but have everything at hand should the need arise. We shall leave this plugged in now. Cell phones may not receive signals during storms." He wrote down the numbers for the infirmary and training center. "Carry your cell phone on your island explorations. So, the cart or a walk?"

Jasirey pushed aside vexation. "Walk." Affection flowing from Liu's hand holding hers, the flower-laced morning breeze, and bird song melted away her irritation.

At the infirmary, Liu drew a blood sample, examined her, then adjusted her spine and hips.

"Liu, if I'm pregnant, you know the odds against it being viable. Let's not tell the people or the boys until we can confirm a healthy pregnancy. Why raise hopes unnecessarily?"

"Ah, precious one, have faith." As she sat up to face him, he leaned back to enjoy the view. "Lovely. Smile at me again." A fist lightly landed against his chest. He kissed it and said, "I have an appointment soon. I shall escort you home."

Jasirey declined. She'd learned to navigate the paths from the infirmary to their cabin, to the market, and to the school.

Sweat dewed her skin by the time she reached the cabin. Lounging on the sofa, she woke to the faint closing bell of the school. As it was wont to do afternoons, the sky darkened. Figuring her sons hadn't remembered to bring umbrellas, Jasirey grabbed two and met them as the first raindrops spattered. It thrilled her to listen to their keen chatter about the day's biology lesson.

"The crocodiles lay eggs in mud and leaves," Michael said. "They let us hold some abandoned babies."

"They'll return them to the river after they grow bigger," Christopher said.

The men joined them soon after the rain. Eyes glowing, they greeted their wife with kisses and lingering hugs.

Jasirey knew she was pregnant. The family walked to the pond where friends dragged off the boys. The men and she swam to the spot shaded by a tree shaped like a weeping willow that Jasirey suspected the people left unoccupied for her. No longer hampered by wounds, she swam strongly and hoped the rush of water over her skin soothed the disquiet flooding her mind.

Ian intercepted and held her drifting by his side. His warm body evoked security—and other things. Jasirey reached under his trunks. The arm around her convulsed. She ran her thumbnail just shy of painful over the head of his penis. Ian gulped air, his arms and legs thrashing to stay afloat.

Recognizing the impish gleam in their wife's eyes, the others pushed the bobbing pair behind the flowering tree and settled them on the ledge jutting out from a natural stone wall. Standing guard, they smothered their laughter at Ian's expense.

He hadn't sufficient blood in his brain to decide between amusement or annoyance. Since Jasirey seemed loath to release him, he chose arousal. Turnabout fair play, Ian wriggled both hands into her bathing suit to remove it and lifted her to straddle him. He reveled in the hot wet heat as he glided inside her with the cool water lapping at his skin. Bodies striving together and apart, waves of sensation roiled to rip tides and drowned them in pleasure. When their bodies came to rest, Jasirey continued stroking softly.

Gently fondling her tender breast, Ian asked, "Was that pure sexual desire, love? It seemed aggressive, perhaps vengeance for the pregnancy?"

Jasirey bolted upright, water splashing and distress storming in her sea blue eyes. "I wasn't thinking that at all."

"Maybe not consciously but possibly feeling it, considering your ambivalence?"

She sniffled.

"Shh, baby. It's all right. There's still time."

"For what?"

"Warming your ass." He caressed that enticing area and kissed her damp face.

❄ ❄ ❄

Jasirey washed the dishes after the dinner her men and boys made while, more a way to connect with them, Christopher and Michael's stepfathers offered homework assistance that the boys didn't need. They had fun discussing bug parts. The night ended with family prayers, and the boys walked unaccompanied to Kharia and Robin's.

The men gathered around their wife on the sofa. Sensing his wife's dread, Fael began. "Loved one, your usually straightforward feelings are muddled tonight."

"You guys believe wholeheartedly in Jasirey's prophecy. I'm sorry. We're courting disaster—miscarriage or physical and mental disabilities." She held up a hand to forestall their objections. "We have the money, the love, to care for a special needs child, but you're not even considering the possibility. The life you envision, want, may not be what you get."

Lee stood abruptly. "You think I'd ever regret our marriage?"

"Not the point. I adore you guys. I'm just not convinced healthy children are possible."

Liu forced his hands to his sides. "You believe our love would wane without children."

Jasirey refused to be deterred. "Children to protect define your purpose and mission. Four men aren't required to care for one woman and two nearly grown boys. Ian has his corporation, wanted me before I came to the Devoted. How will you three adjust to something so much less than you dreamed of?"

16

Ian studied his friends' glaring faces, saw the frisson of fear he hoped Jasirey missed. "Our lady is a sorceress of persuasion," he said casually.

Jasirey's eyes rolled. "I'm being realistic."

"Enough," Lee said through gritted teeth.

Jasirey popped out of her seat. "You keep telling me not to hide my feelings. I can't help it if you don't like them."

Lee grabbed hold with one sharp shake. "You are the most obstinate—" He wrapped her in a steely grip, his kiss urgent, commanding her to submit. Within seconds, he no longer cared which someone submitted to which somebody.

Unbidden tears trickled down Jasirey's cheeks. Lee pulled off her dress and lowered her onto the coffee table. Liu dragged her hips to the edge. She expected demanding and rough. Instead, her men nuzzled, caressed, wiped her tears, and sought to placate as well as stimulate.

"We are yours always," Liu said. "Nothing will pry us from your side." He knelt to taste her damp heat. A devilish gleam entered his eyes. "Gentlemen, sample the allure of pregnancy on our wife."

The husbands slowly circled, fondling along the way. Reaching the apex of her thighs, each dipped in to taste the new development. A flushed face and rising hips indicated Jasirey's appreciation. Lee and Ian lifted to turn her over. Liu grasped her hips, slid in, and thrust gently. Jasirey's breathing quickened. He came and kissed the base of her spine. Lee built on Liu's pace while she gripped the table edge. He also climaxed before she did.

Lifting their wife's tightly wound body, the men draped her over Ian, who lay lengthwise on the table. Not waiting for his guidance, she sheathed him. Fael stood behind, caressed lubricant on himself and between her cheeks, and penetrated an inch. She froze. Fael caressed her curves. Ian suckled her breasts until she moved again as pleasure dictated.

Fael gently rotated his body and eased in and out until Jasirey's telltale signs of an imminent climax became frantic. He withdrew one inch at a time, intensifying her orgasm to mind-reeling heights. Doubts, hurt, and anger drowned as Jasirey shattered in a spray of sun-drenched prisms. She surfaced to petting hands and slow, sweet kisses as the men ensured that her emotional state matched the relaxed contentment of her body.

Fael carefully probed. "I despise the mere idea of you restraining your feelings, beloved. We would never wish that."

Lee cradled her. "I'm a bumbling oaf. Screw us if your feelings bother us."

Jasirey tried to keep her expression prim and proper. "Think I did that."

Lee snorted into her neck.

Jasirey wound fingers through his dreadlocks. "Besides, if we never fought, we'd miss out on spectacular make-up sex." Looking at Fael, she said, "That was different from anything I ever imagined."

Fael kissed her. "It helps that I am more Jasirey-sized. I wished to share the experience with you before the pregnancy makes it uncomfortable."

❧ ❧ ❧

The final week before the family's departure, Jasirey struggled with nausea and dry heaves after the more violent upsets. Liu devised a protein-enriched smoothie she managed to keep down during the worst of it.

Discussing the move one morning, the men broached inviting Robin, a builder, and Kharia, a cook, to join them in the States. "Everett will require assistance," Ian said, "in preparing meals for the people. We might also invite one of the Devoted teachers to continue the island curriculum while maintaining Massachusetts's education regulations."

Jasirey knew both ideas would thrill her sons.

"Kharia and Robin's daughter Zubeena graduates high school this year," Liu said.

"I assumed they only had the boys," Jasirey said. "Who asks them? I don't want it to feel like a command."

"I believe they would appreciate the invitation coming from you," Fael said. "The people are never obligated to do anything for which they are unsuited."

Gray area, Jasirey thought. *Who decided suitability?*

She dropped in on Kharia and Robin that morning. They offered tea, but hoping to walk during the cooler hours and not wanting to take the time, she declined and said, "Our families have become good friends. With all the construction at home and the people living there, we need carpenters and a cook, so I wondered if you'd care to join us in America."

Kharia clasped Jasirey's hand and beamed at her husband.

"Thank you for the honor," Robin murmured. To his wife he said, "We'll talk tonight, then." He bowed jerkily and rushed out for work.

Jasirey's brow furrowed. "Think I scared him."

Kharia squeezed Jasirey's arm. "I think your presence overwhelms him. May I accompany you on your outing?" Their lady's paleness concerned her.

The women meandered and passed a newly fertilized field. Jasirey broke out in a cold sweat. Struggling to retain breakfast, she knelt on the path. "Sorry. Just give me a moment."

Kharia fished out her cell phone to dial the infirmary. Liu was out, but a healer named Niharu left immediately to join Kharia and Jasirey.

Jasirey breathed shallowly through her mouth.

They heard a fast rumbling, and a slight young man pushing a cart appeared on the path. He squatted beside Jasirey. "And how is our little mother?"

Afraid she'd vomit, Jasirey ignored Niharu's breach of privacy. Keeping news of her pregnancy from the people had probably been unrealistic anyway.

Kharia squealed. "Truly? I am so happy."

Niharu's hands skimmed up Jasirey's thighs. "Checking for injuries," he murmured.

"No, she did not fall," Kharia said.

He checked Jasirey's pulse and pupils. "Best we return you home to rest." To Kharia, he said, "You will help me get our lady into the cart."

Jasirey wanted to refuse the officious man but realized walking home wasn't an option.

Niharu took hold of the one-piece handlebar. "I shall see to her now."

"Kharia," Jasirey said, "call Liu, please, and ask him to meet us at the cabin."

"No need to disturb his work." Niharu's eyes drilled into Kharia and turned placating as he looked at Jasirey. "Lie on your left side to aid digestion. I shall have you in bed directly."

Kharia stepped behind Niharu, lifted her phone, and nodded. Niharu set out. Jasirey closed her eyes to hinder conversation. The man had a shrill whistle and kept it up for the entire journey to the cabin. When the jostling and whistling finally stopped, Jasirey sat up. Niharu's arms circled her.

"Come, lady, place your arms around my neck."

Jasirey shuddered.

"Nausea still troubles you. Come."

Jasirey pulled away as his hands molded and turned her body.

"Do not fight me, precious lady."

She smelled his minty breath as his cheek brushed hers and he forced her toward him.

Inches apart, their eyes clashed. Niharu jerked back as though stung.

Liu entered the yard and ran to Jasirey, who attempted to climb out of the cart, her face paler than he'd yet seen it. "Precious one, wait."

Trembling badly, her body slumped onto his.

"Why do you stand there?" he asked Niharu.

"I . . . I attempted . . . "

Liu carried his wife. "Please get the door."

Niharu complied but stayed outside. "I shall care for Jasirey," Liu told him. Niharu appeared dazed, and Liu asked him, "Are you unwell?"

Niharu drew up what height he had. "She is unharmed. Nothing more than nausea." He bowed stiffly and retreated.

The family ate dinner on the patio. Jasirey felt better after a nap though disinclined to discuss the morning's outing and her loss of control with Niharu. She had projected a powerful surge of energy at him to force him to release her and could not get his dazed, confused look out of her mind. She feared that reacting without thinking could cause unintended consequences to others in different situations. Not knowing what consequences or damage she might be capable of especially frightened her.

The men spoke of legal preparations to get everyone to America and of progression on the house. The teens barely uttered a word.

"What's up, guys?" Jasirey asked.

"We're going to miss everybody," Christopher said, "and school."

That was a first. "I'll miss everyone, too. I'm sure your stepdads plan to return often."

"I think," Ian said, "a visit from you three will be anticipated far more than our return."

Jasirey plunked down on his lap. "Aw, poor displaced commander."

Ian flipped her across his knees moments before Robin, Kharia, and their boys approached.

Michael and Christopher jumped up to greet them as did their pink-faced mother.

"We've come for your boys and to answer your invitation," Robin said.

Kharia bubbled over. "We wish to go."

Robin executed a dignified bow.

Jasirey embraced Kharia and shyly hugged Robin, whose blush hid his freckles. "Zubeena is meaning to stay with her grandmother, Kharia's mother, and study nursing," he said.

"He suspects she stays for a boy." Kharia said, hiding a smile at his grimace and lacing her fingers through his. "A nice young man, he reminds me of you," she said to her husband.

Robin grudgingly nodded. Bowing, he, Kharia, and the teenagers headed home.

The men added plans for a duplex outside the compound for Robin, Kharia, and the teacher who would arrive in the States several weeks after the family.

The people threw a farewell party for the family full of laughter, food, and entertainment that impressed Christopher and Michael. They even agreed, without a sign of grudging reluctance, to sing in a group of school friends. The island weaved its spell.

Jasirey decided to impart the news of her pregnancy to her sons before they left the island. She waited anxiously for their reaction.

Michael half pitied and half scoffed. "Come on, Mom. That's all anyone talks about."

❧ ❧ ❧

Jasirey avoided stomach upsets on the flight by drinking Liu's smoothies. A shame she couldn't live on them.

A van waited at her town's small airport to bring the family to a sparsely inhabited nearby area. They turned onto a dirt road dappled by the shade of sprouting spring leaves. Ian planned to widen and pave the narrow lane once the weather guaranteed frost-free nights. The woods opened to fields still sporting the stubble of the previous year's corn crop. Next appeared a grove of white oak, Norway maple, and black cherry and then their home.

Jasirey's breath caught. On either side of the recessed entrance, three stories of multi-paned bay windows stacked one above the other produced the illusion of turrets. Built in stone, the house looked for all the world like a castle.

Everett waited at the wide entrance and greeted the boys affectionately. He had met Fael, Liu, and Lee. He liked them but mourned for what he believed must be Ian's profound loss at finding someone to love and being forbidden to keep her solely for himself. Everett permitted none of his ambivalence to show. Not a member of the Devoted, he wondered what sort of woman agreed to such a marriage.

She looked thinner and unwell. He would concentrate on her health. Addressing her as Jasirey, however, he could not and would not do.

Lee touched fingertips to his lips, then to an ornate mezuzah Fael had sculpted for him. One of the people had attached it to the doorway. It held passages from Deuteronomy—the one and only God ordering his people to keep his commandments.

Inside, a central staircase flanked by gleaming oak balustrades rose to the second-floor balcony. Tall weeping figs filled the bay window alcoves, and doors to the left opened onto a coat closet, a service elevator, a library, and Ian's office.

The living room stretched over most of the right side with long windows facing South and French doors that led to a future flower garden. Norfolk pines and palm lilies flourished in hunter green and navy blue ceramic pots, gleaming in the sun. They complemented furniture upholstered in burgundy striped plaid in blue and green. A fireplace framed in mahogany, the same wood as the polished floor, capped the homeyness Jasirey had envisioned.

At the back of the house sat a dining room and a well-equipped kitchen—a food processor, indoor grill, hanging pots and pans. Jasirey anticipated experimenting with recipes and unfamiliar gadgets.

Ian ushered the family to a door leading outside. He prompted Jasirey through to a room where sun splashed off a wide lap pool and a small whirlpool. The boys whooped. Two changing rooms stood against the interior wall. The other three walls and ceiling consisted of girded glass. Jasirey flung herself into Ian's arms.

"The greenhouse is through the back door," he said.

Jasirey reached up to pull his head down for a kiss, and the boys averted their eyes.

Lee, Liu, and Fael grinned at their wife's infectious delight.

The group went upstairs. On the left, bedrooms for Christopher and Michael and their common room turned out bigger than they'd imagined. The boys hugged Ian without a hint of self-consciousness and stayed to explore while the adults continued their tour.

The back held a corner guest room and en suite bath; one office each for Liu, Fael, and Lee; a bathroom; a staircase to the third floor; and another guest room that mirrored the first. The right hall led to a craft room full of supply cabinets and shelves. Jasirey's boxes of craft supplies sat underneath. The kids missed further kissing and embarrassment.

The craft room adjoined the master bedroom and opened onto a sitting area before a fireplace. Jasirey decided its marble mantle would be the perfect spot for the art pieces Lee and Fael had made for her celebrating her agreement to be Jasirey. At the opposite end lay an even bigger bed than the one in the island's honeymoon cabin.

The third floor housed Everett's bedroom and parlor, a security room for surveillance equipment, and extra rooms for Robin, Kharia, and their boys until workers completed their house.

Jasirey found the absence of a nursery interesting.

Hoping to energize their flagging systems and make it through dinner, the family tried out the pool. Jasirey and her sons had learned to swim in lakes so had skipped diving skills. They admired the men's graceful expertise. Their stepfathers showed the kids the basics, and then Ian, Liu, and the teens broke in the changing-room showers.

Jasirey, Lee, and Fael wrapped up in terry cloth robes to explore the greenhouse. Waiting to be transplanted outside, young tomato, pepper, and other plants requiring longer growing seasons sat on long shelves. Full-grown greens would provide dinner's salad.

The trio decided to shower in the bedroom and found Ian on his laptop at the table in the breakfast nook notifying the island of their safe arrival.

Liu relaxed with a cup of tea.

Jasirey bathed Ian's neck in her tears and murmured, "Sorry," and "It's so wonderful," between breathy sobs.

Liu rubbed their wife's back. "Weariness and hormones."

"Baby." Ian enfolded her in his long arms. Ian appreciated Lee, Liu, and Fael's consideration when they left to check out their offices. He and Jasirey had planned their home. It felt fitting to celebrate it as a couple. He coaxed her into the bathroom and undressed her while waiting for the sunken tub to fill.

It pleased her husbands that instead of being embarrassed, she delighted in her body's growth. Secretly, she liked the smoothing out of her poochy stomach.

Taking advantage of the tub's jets, Ian gently vibrated every inch of Jasirey's body, then used his hands for greater friction until their orgasms rolled in on small but prolonged waves. Ian rocked his wife through the aftershocks and whispered, "You're welcome."

❧ ❧ ❧

Everett brought in breakfast the next morning and, to his shock, found four naked men ranged about a naked Jasirey. The men's hands and arms covered the essentials, yet unable to move, he stood in stunned silence.

Jasirey woke, and her quick intake of breath instantly woke her husbands. She grasped at their arms to prevent them from further uncovering her.

"What?" Ian said. "Oh, Everett. Good God, baby. I thought you were sick."

Everett's rigid, unmoving stance pulled Lee and Liu's attention from Jasirey's cringing body.

Her mortification blasted through Fael, and he rooted for the sheet to cover her.

Everett found his tongue. "Do you wish another tray?"

Ian regarded him closely. "Thank you, Everett. We'll come downstairs."

"Very well." He left without a backward glance.

Fire in his eyes, Lee said, "I think I'll hash this out with Everett."

Jasirey pushed at the men and shrugged on a robe. "Please, stay here." As she left, she flicked tears from her face.

"Not likely," Ian said with a growl. He jumped up and grabbed a pair of slacks. Scowling, he shoved them at Lee.

Fael handed Ian his, and the men sprinted after their wife.

Jasirey cornered Everett in the kitchen. "Ian said you were familiar with the Devoted, Jasirey's legend. Apparently, you have reservations."

Everett's jangled nerves rendered him mute.

"My husbands . . . " The words a deliberate slap, Jasirey dispassionately watched Everett flinch. ". . . are used to the Devoted's acceptance. They don't recognize the disapproval and downright nastiness our family will face."

Restrained by an adamant Fael who wanted to hear Jasirey unfettered from the urge to protect their feelings, the men listened outside the open door.

"Understand, we'll stick together through the slings and arrows. I won't tell my family or most of my friends I have four husbands. They'd judge me a whore, too."

Everett stepped back, hit a counter, and clutched at it. "I never thought that."

"Sure you did. Normal human reaction."

The words sounded benign, but Everett's mouth went dry.

"We'll have to weather outside disapproval," Jasirey said, "but not from those we allow close. Ian loves you, counts on your support. I won't let you hurt him, Lee, Liu, or Fael."

When she finally diverted her gaze, Everett found himself able to release the counter.

Jasirey's eyes remained dry, but tears welled in her voice. "If you can't accept us, our family, I will ask you to leave."

Ian and Lee pushed into the room as Everett grasped her frigid hands. He chafed at them, intent on the woman who appeared so small and fragile. He'd met no one more protective or indomitable.

"My dear . . . Jasirey. You are a singular person, although you remind me of my departed wife. I believe she'd have been very fond of you. We shall muddle along fine." Everett drew her close as she trembled with barely audible tears. Berating himself for hurting her, he determined no one else would ever do so on his watch.

He cleared his throat. "Gentlemen, please seat your wife while I prepare breakfast."

Everett soon became accustomed to constant—to his British sensibilities—touching and kissing among the adults, even to the men sprawled around their wife each morning. At least they had the good sense to cover her. He might not voice it, but Everett found their evident devotion rather sweet.

Jasirey loved Everett for his thoughtfulness in soliciting her advice, despite not needing it, on the daily running of the house. Morning sickness, sometimes lasting twenty-four hours, too often incapacitated her. She was grateful he took up the slack.

Thus far unable to summon the courage to explain her multiple husbands to Lizzie, her friend of twenty years who had been with her on a trip to Vermont where they met Ian and who had cheered on the couple toward a relationship, Jasirey decided to schedule a lunch date. She drove to her friend's house in a small fuel-efficient car that Ian futilely advised she trade for a heavier, safer vehicle. Lizzie was bound to get loud, so Jasirey planned to tell her in the car.

Lizzie brought up the subject for her. "A mansion and he decked you out in bling." She fingered Jasirey's bracelet. "That's some piece of hardware. An engagement present? Have you and Mr. Hunky set the date?"

"We kind of already got married on the island."

"What? Kind of? Is it legal here?"

Harder to explain than Jasirey anticipated, no matter how she phrased them, the facts sounded ludicrous. "We aren't married legally, but according to island tradition, I'm married to Ian . . . and three others—Lee, Liu, and Fael." Suddenly grateful she hadn't had to explain that to her sons, Jasirey raced past Lizzie's incredulous goggling. "I can't tell you much unless I have your word you won't repeat it to anyone."

Lizzie smirked. "You're pranking me."

"No. Ian belongs to a group who searches for and aids a woman who's supposed to . . . to bestow a better world on the future through her children. They think I'm her."

Lizzie's eyes narrowed. "A cult?"

"No one's forced to join or stay or do anything not in their best interest, including me."

"So why the multiple guys?"

"They believe managing her care and her children's requires more than one. It disappointed them I chose only four."

"Good God, Shannon. I can't believe Ian wants to share you. What's he thinking? What are you thinking, going along?"

"They mean everything to me. Ian brought me to these people fully aware of the possible consequences. He believed I was this woman long before I accepted it."

Hung up on the multiple husbands, Lizzie failed to register the children part. At lunch, Jasirey let her friend change the subject to her ongoing battle to move from the past as a married woman and build something new as a widow she didn't want but that life required. Before dropping Lizzie off, Jasirey invited her to come see the house and meet her husbands.

"You say you're happy, Shan, but . . . . Just give me some time, okay?"

Satisfied she hadn't been rejected outright, Jasirey hugged Lizzie goodbye.

Later, Ian arrived home and stopped by his wife's craft room to ask about her lunch with Lizzie.

"It threw her," Jasirey said. "She needs time to process before visiting."

Jasirey's resignation seemed no better than being hurt or sad. Everett and then Lizzie—her warning of reactions outside the Devoted glared at Ian.

Doubt Ebbs

Robin, Kharia, their boys, and the teacher arrived and took up residence on the third floor. Groundskeepers and housekeepers accompanied them and stayed at the dormitory where Kharia directed meal planning and preparation. Those living there oversaw serving and cleanup of evening meals to allow Kharia to join her family for dinner at the main house.

Ian set up medical proxies to ensure everyone had access to information in case of emergencies. Thinking it time for an ultrasound for Jasirey, he asked acquaintances in the medical field to recommend an obstetrician. The husbands chose one in Boston. Jasirey argued for an ob-gyn closer to home, but the men refused to budge.

"He specializes in older women and at-risk pregnancies," Ian said. "He's what is called a concierge doctor. We pay a retainer for him to provide enhanced care such as home visits, especially as you get bigger and traveling becomes more difficult for you. Our agreement includes use of the plane when he travels here."

Jasirey knew the prophecy of quadruplets had them concerned for her health more than usual. Unconvinced of the likelihood of that and not in the mood to argue, she remained silent.

"This doctor has also agreed to allow me," Liu said, "to act as part of your care team in an unofficial capacity, of course. He respects holistic medicine."

Jasirey smiled at her men. "Have to admit, he sounds ideal."

Ian scheduled a Monday appointment and, for the Saturday before, a private marriage ceremony and public reception in Boston to introduce his wife to business associates. His Boston house too small to accommodate everyone, he booked several suites at the hotel where the reception would be held.

Cuddling her men in the bedroom, Jasirey said, "My parents agreed to come, since we can send the plane for them."

Her parents had moved to South Carolina after retirement to escape heating costs in the Northeast.

Ian said, "I'll send a car to take them to the airport."

She kissed him in thanks. "My sisters plan to drive in together from New Jersey. The youngest, Natalie, won't ask her husband to skip work to attend a frivolous party. He squirrels away every extra cent for retirement. No kids. She won't tell him that she and our middle sister, Marcie, will spend the weekend shopping for bargains." Jasirey grinned. "Bet Marcie asked Paul, her husband, to stay home with their daughter."

"Will you join them on this shopping spree?" Lee asked, thinking about security.

Her merriment ebbed. "Not much of a shopper. Besides, can't think of a thing I need."

"Do you have a dress for the party?" Ian asked.

Crap. "You know I don't."

Fael ran a hand over her hair. "Might not your sisters help you with that?"

"They're eleven months apart. I'm a decade older. Different tastes."

"And?" Fael persisted, unwilling to let the subject drop.

Jasirey shrugged, then sighed at his implacable stare. "And you want my life story."

The men cocooned her.

"I grew up in New Jersey. My mom suffers from bipolar disorder and depression. She slept through most of my early childhood. One hour to the next, you never knew whether she'd consider you wonderful or the bane of her existence.

"In my parents' families, the older kids took care of themselves and the younger ones. My mother and father had four kids and continued the tradition, which suited me. I preferred being alone. It was peaceful in my head. My dad hadn't bargained for such a volatile wife. Like me, he withdrew into his own world and spoke to us kids only to deliver an order or to criticize. They expected us to kiss their cheeks at bedtime. I don't remember any in return."

Fael sensed something darker edging in on the sadness.

"It was my job to take the girls outside after school. At two and three, they could barely walk in their snowsuits. Acres of woods backed our street of houses. One day, I hid behind the trees and waited for them to cry before showing myself again."

"Sounds like a typical kid," Lee said.

"Except I did it several times."

Such cringing shame. Fael cradled her head on his shoulder. "Why, loved one?"

"The hugs. They grabbed hold like they never wanted to let go."

Jasirey's childhood was the antithesis of the men's—even Fael who, though impoverished, had known family affection and stability. The men massaged her neck and lower back where she held her tension.

"I told them about you, Ian. They wouldn't accept the rest of you guys."

"We'll deal," Lee said. "You said four kids?"

"I had a brother, Charlie, two years younger, diagnosed with schizophrenia and paranoia in his late teens. Medication was a trial-and-error business then, maybe still today. He'd feel better, stop his medications or, more often, believe he was being poisoned or that the government conspired against him." Her eyes clouded. "I'd visit him in the psych ward, find him sitting in a hallway, a drooling idiot, unable to function. He hated the drugs. I couldn't blame him.

"After I married, before the boys were born, he died, crashed into a tree. Maybe intentionally."

The men caressed in wordless consolation.

"They hospitalized my mom for a few months. My brother was her favorite—smart, funny, really likeable when his subconscious wasn't taunting him. I miss him." She attempted a smile. "He reveled in bullying my sisters. His illness embarrassed them, and they despised him. No funeral. I spread his ashes on a lake near the town where our family camped every year for vacation when we were young. One of my few happy family memories."

Ian measured his next question. "When we first arrived on the island, Esias, an elderly man with dementia, approached you about being Jasirey before the Devoted could explain who she is and that you were a candidate to be her, our lady. You were naturally perturbed that I'd brought you there without telling you why."

Jasirey pulled her knees to her chest. "That's one way of putting it."

"Yes, well." Ian's hand skimmed over his shaved head. "There seemed more to your reaction. You were terrified—we think more of the frail old man himself than what he said. Will you tell us what prompted your fear?"

When she was eight years old, age-spotted hands with raised blue veins skimmed and furtively reached under her bathrobe. "I was a pretty child," she said, the words flat facts, "confused by attention I didn't understand, scared because I couldn't prevent it and stay safe."

Ian's encircling arms tightened. "You had no one you trusted to tell?"

"I believed I'd be blamed, my fault. One benefit of getting fat, the attention stopped." She drew in a breath, released it. "According to Kai, the past prepared me to be Jasirey. It's all good." She nudged the subject back to her family.

"I was an excellent student. My sisters resented being compared to me by other family adults and teachers, which of course wasn't fair, especially considering the age difference. Kids at school resented me, too. At assemblies, the teachers placed me between the boisterous kids. If I got sucked into their fun, one disapproving look set me straight, and I'd do my job."

Lee glowered. "Which was to make the adults' lives easier."

"Do your sisters now realize," Fael said, "that you mothered them?"

Jasirey poked his ribs. "You're peeking."

"I did not need my empathic senses. It is a logical conclusion from the age difference between you and your sisters and from your mother's debilitation with her illness." His eyes glowed with love. "You have a strong tendency to protect."

Jasirey smiled. "Marcie, maybe, since having her daughter." Her brow furrowed. "Something's up with her. Short phone calls or no answer. I'll ask this weekend."

Lee cradled his little one's face. "Always the caregiver. And who cared for you?"

❧ ❧ ❧

At the Boston hotel a few weeks later, Ian's admin Charlotte clasped her hands together, bowed, and laughed at their lady's surprise. "I assume Ian neglected to tell you I'm a member of the Devoted. He needed someone in the office familiar with our mission. I'm pleased to assist you in finding a gown for the reception."

Two security people accompanied the women to a boutique specializing in evening wear.

Jasirey winced at the prices.

The sales clerk huffed. "Such short notice, tailoring is impossible. We must find something that fits." She gave Jasirey's figure a critical gaze and sighed. "I have only two dresses for the full-figured."

Jasirey suppressed a snide remark.

Charlotte's eyes twinkled. "Alice, if anyone can pull off a miracle, it's you."

"Maybe." She glared at a fuchsia dress on a nearby mannequin and studied Jasirey's ivory skin and unusual eyes. "I think this one complements your coloring, but it has sleeves." That seemed to offend Alice.

"I prefer sleeves," Jasirey said, which didn't appease the sales clerk.

She pointed at Charlotte. "Your dress is ready. Try it on." She escorted Jasirey to a dressing room the size of her old bedroom. "Clothes off. I'll fetch the dress."

Alice about-faced before Jasirey's protest made it past her lips. She stripped down to her underwear. That was all the woman would get.

Carrying in a large garment bag, Alice glanced at Jasirey. "Bra." She hung up the dress threaded in gold and shimmering from burgundy to plum.

"Alice." Charlotte's voice floated over walls that ended a foot below the ceiling. "I need your expert eye, please."

The salesclerk huffed once again and pointed at Jasirey's bra. After she left, Jasirey scurried out of it and into the dress. She easily dragged it up her body but struggled with the zipper.

A beefy man with one-tone brown hair entered. Grass green eyes took in Jasirey's predicament. "May I?" A finger skimmed up her back. "Perfect fit. Come out to the main room. The mirrors are larger." He gently grasped Jasirey's elbow.

The polite "May I?" clashed with the insistent hand on Jasirey's arm. She tried to disengage. Eerie eyes mocked.

"Something wrong?"

Jasirey's gaze remained level. "Let's ask my security people."

The man's other hand rose to rest on her belly. His eyes glinted as hers fired. "No need. I think we'll wait, oh, say six months. Tell Ian Marcus says hello."

"Well?" Strafe asked as Marcus climbed into the rented sedan.

"Yes, neither Madonna nor whore." Strafe knew either bored him. "She's pregnant."

Strafe gaped. Ian's woman had seen Strafe while spying on Ian in Vermont, so Marcus had ordered the younger man to stay in the car. As no other female had sunk a claw into Strafe, his fascination with her intrigued Marcus.

Bent on revenge against Ian and his team for interfering in his human trafficking business, he kept tabs on Ian through Strafe's computer skills and knew he lived in Boston with the woman. Marcus had business in the area offloading one shipment and picking up another and had decided to take a peek at her.

He considered Jasirey a formidable woman, but even the strongest crumbled with a child at stake. Marcus wanted his contest of wills with her focused solely between them, a delicious side benefit to using her against Ian. Besides, he had no obstetric facilities, and dealing in infants presented far too many headaches. Never allowing impatience to sway him, he would wait.

"Back to the ship," Marcus said. Scanning the rearview mirror, Strafe pulled out slowly. "You'll see her again. Best we aren't seen now."

Strafe immediately obeyed the veiled warning.

Charlotte's fearful reaction to Marcus's name had Alice stammering apologies. Jasirey patted her heaving shoulders and bought the burgundy gown.

After a hasty return to the hotel, Ian, Lee, and Fael left the women in the sitting room with Liu as they contacted the island from one of the bedrooms. Jasirey simmered when Liu sidestepped her questions.

Charlotte played peacemaker. "Your husbands have run across Marcus on several missions. He is wanted in numerous countries."

"Precious one," said Liu, "trust us to keep you safe."

33

A hot gleam in her eyes warned Liu his wife would expect an in-depth answer later.

Jasirey went to dress up a bit for dinner with her family. Well, to pacify her mother, who hated Jasirey's preferred casual attire. Ian had suggested a private dining room. She chose the public one. Sitting amidst strangers might restrain her family's behavior.

Jasirey joined her mother, Anne; father, Richard; and sisters in the hotel foyer. She returned her father's kiss on the mouth, which she disliked but tolerated so as not to offend him. She once tried to explain that other female relatives offered their cheeks to keep their lipstick intact rather than because, as he believed, they were stuck-up.

While introducing her family to Ian and then to Liu, Fael, and Lee as security personnel, Jasirey realized she hadn't prepared her men for certain prejudices.

Apple-shaped like her mother, Natalie eyed the three foreigners. "Must be the frigging UN at your place."

"I liked Roger," Anne said. "He was sweet. Always called me Mom."

"Not as successful, though," Natalie said snidely. "Private jets come in handy."

Jasirey stole a glance at her dumbfounded men. "Shall we order?"

Her father opened the menu and closed it. "Don't worry about it," her mother said. "He's rich."

Anne ordered seafood chowder and a lobster and prime rib dinner.

Natalie followed suit and picked up the wine list.

Jasirey shook her head at her sister. She knew her diabetic mother could not afford alcohol on top of the carb rich dinner she had ordered. Anne, however, would indulge if Natalie did.

Natalie grudgingly set the list down.

Marcie, who had lost substantial if not too much weight, ordered grilled shrimp and salad.

Jasirey chose duck with plum sauce, a favorite of her father's. He ordered the same.

Happy that the restaurant had sugar-free apple pie, Anne observed Ian with slightly more favor. "I once dreamed that Shannon, with all her brains, would be the millionaire of the family. Guess marrying into it is as good."

Jasirey inhaled a sip of iced tea. Ian patted her back as she coughed.

Conversation centered on Ian's business and assets for a relatively disaster-free dinner. The waiter delivered the check, and Richard fished out his wallet. "I'll leave the tip."

"Don't be stupid," Anne said.

Jasirey smiled at him. "Don't worry about it, really."

"We're happy you agreed to be our guests," Ian said. He rose to assist Jasirey out of her chair. The others helped her mother and sisters.

Jasirey hid a grin at their astonishment. Returning her family to their rooms, she hugged her parents. Natalie pulled her aside as Ian said good night. "We need to talk to you—without him."

Marcie refused to meet her older sister's eyes.

"Ian, I'll visit my sisters for a while."

He kissed her forehead. "Call before you leave the room."

Natalie and Marcie perched across from each other on their beds.

Marcie still hadn't looked at Jasirey. She sat beside her younger sister and bumped shoulders. "What's up, kid?"

"Your new husband seems nice."

"I like him."

"I want to get an early start at the shops tomorrow," Natalie said. "Get on with it."

Marcie grabbed a tissue from the nightstand. "I've done something stupid I don't want Paul to find out about."

"The gambling," Jasirey said. "You haven't stopped."

"He'll divorce me."

Jasirey knew Paul had zero tolerance for what he considered self-indulgent behavior and became ballistic at the waste of money. According to him, addiction was nothing but an excuse.

"How much?"

"I only went to the casino a couple of times."

Jasirey said nothing.

Marcie's tears fell faster. Finally, "Twenty thousand."

"What do you intend to do about it?"

Marcie's eyes snapped to Jasirey.

Natalie puffed up. "You know you've got the money. Stop acting so high and mighty. You're still nothing but a housewife."

"Shut up," Marcie said, her voice barely audible.

"She just wants to see you grovel."

"Don't be stupid." Marcie reached for her older sister's hand. "I'm scared."

Jasirey squeezed lightly and felt Marcie relax a bit. "Money won't solve the underlying problem," Jasirey said.

"I know." She dabbed her eyes. "I'll go to the program you told me about."

"Good. Give the therapist permission to tell me when you're doing better, and I'll help you with the debt." Jasirey clasped both of Marcie's hands. "You need long-term support, probably weekly meetings and therapy. You should tell Paul." She smiled at her sister's panic. "We'll talk to him together."

"I'll never understand it." Marcie's lips crooked. "He's not afraid of anyone, except you."

Because I'm the bigger bully, Jasirey thought, her smile fixed.

The next evening, the husbands whistled at their gorgeous wife. Her new dress scintillated, but their attention riveted on her face. They'd never seen her in makeup. A smoky look enhanced her blue-spruce eyes. Stunning. The dress had required a deeper shade of lip color, and the men wanted to nibble on the succulent result.

Ian handed her a flat box hinged on one end. Jasirey stared at the necklace and earrings of fire opals surrounded by rubies and diamonds. The necklace nestled prettily against her cleavage. Tears glittered with the diamonds.

Clinging to her men, Jasirey said, "It's a little scary. Thought I was so independent. Don't think I could survive now without you guys."

She had to reapply her lipstick before the judge, a friend of Ian's who doubled as a pastor, performed the marriage ceremony in their suite.

Afterward, Ian escorted Jasirey and her family to the reception in the hotel banquet room. He inserted himself between his wife and Natalie, whose rapacious eyes remained fastened on Jasirey's necklace.

Liu, Lee, and Fael disappeared into the crowd. They seemed unfazed, but it hurt Jasirey not to be able to acknowledge them. Ian settled her family at a table and offered his arm to steer her toward group after group. Names and faces blurred.

Her golden skin the color of tea with lemon showcased to perfection in a pale yellow gown, Charlotte introduced her date, a young woman who became tongue-tied in Ian's presence. Charlotte sent him a look, and he engaged the young lady in conversation.

"Too young for me, and I don't date employees," Charlotte said to Jasirey, "but she needed assurance that her sexual orientation has no bearing on her job."

"Very effective and kind," Jasirey said, hugging her.

Jasirey returned to the table and sympathized with her father's aggravated expression. Formal parties galvanized her mother. Socializing in general annoyed her father. She preferred small get-togethers herself and conversations that gave a glimpse behind the social façade.

She enjoyed her mother and sisters' excitement at the multi-course meal, which required several fork and spoon changes. Orchestra members began taking their seats during the dessert course.

Jasirey skipped the tiramisu. Her nerves fluttered despite her husbands' dancing lessons.

In a nod to tradition, Ian led her onto the floor for the first dance. Halfway through, silver clinked against crystal. Ian dipped Jasirey and captured her mouth in a kiss that drew cheers.

Ian danced with Jasirey's mother and sisters while a throng of his business associates claimed Jasirey.

Talking nonstop, Trevor bounced her around the floor. "I had a feeling about you two. Even Fran agreed, and here you are. I'm glad."

Jasirey had met Trevor and Fran at the Vermont resort where they conducted training for Ian's corporation. Trevor's awkward sincerity touched her.

Liu, Fael, and Lee each managed a dance with their wife, who started to pale in fatigue. Lee's glower fended off further interested males as he escorted Jasirey to a quiet corner.

Ian joined them, leading a perfectly highlighted blond matron in a coral designer suit. She clasped his arm in easy familiarity. Two younger women in miniscule black dresses trailed in their wake.

"Meredith, my wife, Shannon. Meredith is a long-time friend of the family."

Meredith's daughters focused their attention on the three exotic, yummy men.

Jasirey greeted the older woman, who coolly extended her hand. Jasirey didn't bother to engage in conversation. It required no sixth sense to recognize what ran through Meredith's mind. Figuring it was good practice, Jasirey left Lee, Fael, and Liu to their own devices with the daughters, though her poor husbands appeared at a loss.

Ian leaned in and whispered, "Worms on a hook."

Jasirey laughed.

Meredith's brown eyes narrowed in a delicate sneer. "Your mother seems exceedingly proud of your fine marital catch."

Debating whether to declaw the catty woman, Jasirey decided she didn't care enough to cause a fuss. Meredith hadn't asked a question, so she ignored her.

The older woman's eyes glittered. "Your mother also speaks highly of your talents. Is your wife a chanteuse, Ian?"

"She has a lovely voice but is not a performer," Ian said in quiet tones.

"Gallant and politic—shrewd."

Oh, what the hell. "I haven't sung for my mother in a long time," Jasirey said.

Annoyed at Meredith's goading and at Jasirey for giving in to it, Ian searched her eyes. "You really want to sing, baby?"

"I think so. Weird, huh?"

Ian led the group to the orchestra conductor before Jasirey's nerves caught up to her bravado. He admitted to the petty satisfaction he'd gain at Jasirey putting Meredith in her place.

Fael, Liu, and Lee's thoughts ran along similar lines as they strove for some polite way to unclamp the daughters from their arms.

Not used to an orchestra, Jasirey asked for a piano accompaniment. A safe presence, her men stood below the foot-high stage. They liked her voice.

Jasirey chose a favorite Barbra Streisand classic.

Her voice soared with a power and range the husbands hadn't realized their wife possessed.

A crowd gathered, entranced by Jasirey's expressive passion. The conductor brought in the orchestra for a soaring crescendo. Jasirey finished on a sweet note that lingered on the acoustically perfect air as she left the stage before the cheering audience could call for another song.

Meredith's arm slinked through Ian's. "Her first marriage surprised her relatives."

Coming up behind Meredith and her daughters with their glittering eyes, Jasirey crowded them into the midst of her men. "Yes, they thought I was gay."

"What?" Ian snorted on a disbelieving laugh.

"According to your sister Natalie," Meredith said, "they still do."

Only Jasirey's husbands noted the fleeting pain in her eyes.

"Give it up, Meredith. I daresay you had your daughters inflict their best shot on Ian. He's a smart man. He chose me."

Meredith's voice vibrated. "Defy me at your risk, dear."

"We don't move in the same circles of entitlement, dear, and I'm sure we both prefer it that way. Excuse us. This is too 1960s to be entertaining."

Ian nestled Jasirey against him. "Ladies." He guided Jasirey away.

Lee, Liu, and Fael followed with face-splitting grins.

"I should feel bad," Jasirey said. "That was really aimed at Natalie." She grinned back at her foolish husbands. "But I won't."

Bubbling with pride, Anne patted her daughter's face. "I haven't heard you sing in years. Wasn't she wonderful, Richard?"

His mouth thinned. Jasirey had always wondered if perhaps he felt called upon to balance his wife's gushing. He rarely praised.

Later, in their suite, Fael asked, "Why does your family believe you to be homosexual?"

"My Uncle David's kids, he has a daughter my age. She seemed everything I wasn't, adventurous, daring, and rebellious instead of shy. I took studiousness and responsibility to the point of missing my childhood. I loved and admired her. I think openly expressed love confused her. Her parents discouraged displays of emotion."

Jasirey shrugged. "In our teens, I realized my cousin's bravado masked equal insecurities, maybe greater inhibitions in expressing herself. I guess labeling me as gay was her confidence booster. Or maybe the fact that I rarely dated caused the rumors. I'd be interested in a guy who wouldn't be interested in a fat woman, or guys who seemed attracted did nothing for me." She kissed Fael's cheek. "Maybe I was saving up for you guys."

❦ ❦ ❦

Jasirey's sisters checked out the next morning. The family had a late lunch with her parents and saw them off in Ian's small plane at a local airport. "You be good to my daughter," Anne said to Ian.

"Always my plan." He kissed his mother-in-law's cheek and shook Richard's hand.

Before going to Boston, the family had agreed that Lee and Fael would return home by car after the party.

Four men would be too many to descend on the obstetrician who met Jasirey, Ian, and Liu in his private, upscale office on Monday. He ushered them to a large sitting area containing two couches that faced each other.

The doctor gazed sternly at Jasirey. "Considering the higher risk of complications you and the child face, I'm wondering why you waited this long for an appointment."

"May I call you by your first name?" Jasirey asked the doctor in an effort to restrain a bristling Ian.

The doctor stumbled momentarily at the unexpected request. "Of course. Jesse."

"Jasirey."

Ian and Liu exchanged glances. Their wife rarely referred to herself as Jasirey. They suspected she'd taken command.

"We've been out of the country. Liu's a well-trained medic."

The doctor reviewed Jasirey's medical history with her. "I'll send you to the examination room and our midwife for the physical. Then I believe you have an appointment for an ultrasound." Liu nodded. "We can meet back here after lunch to discuss everything."

The midwife performed the physical with gently efficient hands. "You say you're twelve weeks along," she said. "The size of your uterus suggests longer." She placed a stethoscope on Jasirey's abdomen. "Your history reports two single births."

40

"Yes. What do you hear?"

The woman patted Jasirey's shoulder. "Let's wait for the ultrasound."

Jasirey rejoined Ian and Liu and followed the midwife's directions to the radiology department in the adjoining hospital. The busy weekend had exacted a toll on Jasirey, and Liu insisted that she rest in the waiting room instead of pacing. An aide ushered them into a room half an hour later and asked Jasirey to lie on a gurney, a cloth draped over her naked lower half. The technician came in, went through preliminaries, and started the ultrasound.

Ian had no idea what to expect on the screen. He manfully suppressed a cringe as the technician inserted a phallic-shaped wand into his wife. A blurry shadow appeared and resolved into a head followed by a tiny body, heart visibly beating. Incredible.

Another movement attracted the technician's attention, and she maneuvered the wand. A second little body became visible, a third to Jasirey's soft, "Oh," and then a fourth. The men hugged each other and their radiant wife.

Caught up in the wonder of quadruplets, the technician paid little attention to the adults. "Do you want to know the sexes?"

They had chosen beforehand to be surprised. The technician took time getting measurements of each fetus and views from different angles for the doctor before handing Jasirey pictures to take home.

Ian and Liu brought their very pregnant lady to lunch while waiting for the return appointment with Jesse, scheduled for the same day because of the distance they traveled.

Jasirey wanted to skip and twirl, not sit and eat. Her men threatened to chain her to the chair. She managed minestrone and salad as, radiating joy, she smiled non-stop throughout the meal. Other diners smiled back as her contagious joy filled them with warmth.

On their walk back to the office, the men noticed pedestrians halting to stare at their joyous wife. No one became annoyed at others blocking the sidewalks.

❈ ❈ ❈

Quadruplets without in vitro fertilization also excited Jesse. "A pregnancy for the record books. Congratulations."

41

He shook Ian's hand. Jasirey's unfettered smile dazzled him. A disconcerting attraction heightened into warm familiarity when her small hand engaged his. Staring into eyes the color of blue spruce trees, Jesse awkwardly released her.

"Are you married?" Jasirey asked.

"Yes. Our twenty-fifth anniversary this year, two kids—a girl and a boy—both out of college, on their own. My daughter's a physical therapist. My son prefers accounting, his mother's profession." Jesse realized he was babbling. "The babies appear healthy and on target for twelve weeks."

"We must inform you of our circumstances," Liu said, "so you may effectively treat Jasirey. According to our tradition, she married four men of different races."

Apparently, Jesse had not heard it all during his busy career. He knew, of course, that polygamist groups existed and that polyamorous groups had become more popular. A woman with multiple husbands, however, was still unusual. He wouldn't judge and took a moment to choose an innocuous question. "What symptoms have you experienced?"

Liu answered. "She has lost five pounds and suffers frequent nausea." He described the treatments used.

Jesse agreed he should continue them. At the next appointment, if Jasirey had not gained the prescribed weight, they would discuss other options.

"Our family requires discretion," Jasirey said. "No journals or medical papers."

"The law and the standard practice of this office guarantee confidentiality." The pretty sound of her laugh pricked a hole in Jesse's bubbling annoyance.

"I'm afraid there's more to our story than you're prepared to believe right now. I hope you'll agree to get to know us and be our family's friend as well as my doctor."

Jesse leaned back on his chair and almost hit his head on the bookcase behind him. Jasirey's eyes softened. He had the eerie feeling she guessed quite a few of his discordant thoughts.

"Will you visit, meet my husbands, before you decide?"

Jesse rested his elbows on his desk. He liked the woman and suspected his wife would, too. "I'll speak to my wife."

❧ ❧ ❧

Jasirey slept most of the trip home. When she saw the people—household staff, groundskeepers, builders—forming a reception line halfway up the driveway, she said, "I'd like to get out and show everyone the ultrasound pictures."

The people threw flowers and heaped blessings on their most precious lady. Lee swung her through the air, and an ecstatic Fael rained kisses on her face.

Released from school, Christopher and Michael met their mother in the craft room. Though they needed no confirmation of her pregnancy, they waited for what else she had to say.

"You guys okay with all the fuss?"

"Is it a boy or girl?" Michael asked.

"We decided to be surprised. Odds are there will be both."

That piqued Michael's interest.

"Brace yourselves," she told them as she raised four fingers.

"You're kidding" and "Holy shit" exploded from the boys. She ignored the latter.

"Everybody's excited that you're pregnant, but . . ." Christopher shrugged. ". . . you're older. Can't that cause problems?"

Jasirey had to walk a line, hoping neither to lie nor unduly alarm them. "Babies of older parents run higher risks for birth defects. The doctor's checking. The ultrasound looks normal."

The boys knew what that was. She'd shown them their pictures often enough.

"Your stepdads and I believe they'll be healthy." Jasirey's smile blazed. She did believe it.

After chocolate milk scented hugs, she sent the boys off and used her new confidence to phone the next person on the short list of people she could talk to about her pregnancy, whose reaction was pure Lizzie and comfortingly familiar in a life far outside what Jasirey used to consider normal.

"Holy jumping Hannah. On purpose? You realize how old you'll be when it graduates?"

"When they graduate."

"Twins?" A snicker from Jasirey. Lizzie managed a wheezing squeak. "Three?"

"Quadruplets."

Complete silence for two seconds. "Are you insane? Never mind. Do I get to be godmother?"

"I'll ask the fathers."

"Good, God. Guess I'll have to meet them. Shan, Ian really accepts this?"

"Ask him. Lizzie, I can't tell my family, probably not my friends. You're my closest friend and look at the difficulty you're having."

"I won't lie. Four husbands give me the heebie-jeebies. But I've always been able to count on you. And same goes here."

❧ ❧ ❧

The celebration dinner consisted of Jasirey's favorites—turkey, the usual sides, and an apple-date cake with peanut butter frosting. Touched by his effort to please her, she kissed Everett's cheeks. He ate at the family table, his best gift to her.

Afterward, the husbands suggested a walk. Transformed, the garden burst with lilacs, candy-colored tulips, and purple and yellow pansies. Leaf-patterned iron benches dotted flagstone paths, all of which converged on a stone-bordered waterfall flowing into a pond inhabited by mottled white, orange, and black koi. They followed Jasirey's fingers trailing in the water.

When gnats joined them, Ian brought Jasirey to his office to contact the Imperiat.

"Dearest one, blessings on you," Master Kai said.

Jasirey peered at him shyly. "I believe now."

"So I see." Their lady's glow created an answering brightness in his heart. "I shall inform the people, which will no doubt prompt our own celebration."

He also informed her that Satoko and Mashita were prepared to join the family at her discretion.

Pleased to have the couple's assistance in setting up the nursery, Jasirey asked that they come as soon as they were ready. She spoke to

Kai for a bit longer before, finally free from distractions, she went to their bedroom to face her husbands with stubborn determination.

"Marcus," Jasirey said, "obviously wants to pay you back for something, and I was a handy target. Why did he walk away?"

Both of Ian's hands scrubbed over his head. "Baby, believe me, he won't get near you again."

"Guys, I trust you implicitly, but forewarned is forearmed. I want to help myself, be on alert, avoid dangerous situations. I need to know the danger to do that."

They couldn't deny their wife's logic or demand for information. Lee glowered anyway. "Marcus traffics humans—slaves—mostly for the sex trade."

"That makes no sense," Jasirey said. "I'm worthless in that market."

Lee shuddered and enfolded Jasirey in massive arms that he wished were adequate to always keep her safe.

Revenge against them—the husbands could think of no other reason why Marcus would accost their wife.

Sensing deep unease in her men, Jasirey willed her body to relax and felt their tension begin to wane. "Let's put it aside. I trust you guys, and we're celebrating." She mimed a huge baby belly. "Guess I can stop feeling guilty that my lovely men have done most of the work in this marriage."

The men stilled. *Damn.* Jasirey hated it when they got pissed at what she intended as a simple, factual observation. "It's just that I made all the decisions in my first marriage."

Fael's gold eyes flared. "Do we not seek your input concerning family decisions?"

"Yes, because you're excellent husbands. This is my adjustment problem. You seek my input versus needing it."

"You think we don't need you?" Lee's voice dropped to a dangerous growl.

Jasirey plopped facedown into a pillow. "Not what I meant, and I don't want to fight, not tonight."

With as close to a whine as they'd ever heard from her, the men relented.

Lee patted her fanny. "Little one, maybe we're letting this Marcus business get to us, but are you truly unaware of everything you give us?"

"The fullness of our lives because of you?" Liu turned her to face them.

"Beloved," Fael said, "you see me as no one else before. I am blessed."

Ian tapped the tip of her nose. "Got it?"

"My saps, I love you all so."

New Friends

Jasirey paid for her overindulgence at dinner by feeling sick most of the night. She encouraged the men to go to their offices for some uninterrupted sleep. Concerned their earlier argument had caused her upset, they adamantly refused. Liu used acupuncture to ease the nausea. Still, she couldn't face solid food the next day and spent the morning in bed.

Ian had installed an intercom weeks before to page Everett when they were ready for breakfast and thereby prevent his walking in on them in the middle of sex. They left it on for Everett to monitor Jasirey from the kitchen.

In the afternoon, to assure Christopher and Michael they were available for them, the stepfathers challenged them and Bazir and Kirani to pool volleyball. They maintained a close score for pride's sake but did not hand the teens a win.

On retiring for the night, Fael laid a light blanket over their wife. Lee placed a bucket at the foot of the bed in case the bathroom proved too far.

Jasirey woke in the nightlight-lit room to the sensation of ants crawling on her legs and inside her body. She pushed off the blanket and resisted getting up but couldn't lie still. Lee lay sleeping on his back beside her, blocking the easiest way off the bed. Easing herself over him, she started to shake uncontrollably.

Lee's eyes flew open and saw Jasirey, her nightshirt clinging to her, damp with sweat. He shouted Liu's name. Breathing hard, she reached for Lee, but eyes blurred, she collapsed.

"What the hell's happening?" Ian gathered Jasirey, head lolling, against his chest.

Liu checked her pulse and pupils. Suspecting low blood sugar, he asked Lee to fetch a pitcher of juice. Fael left a message on Jesse's cell phone. Lee returned with the juice, and Liu cupped Jasirey's small chin and tipped a glass to her lips. Much of the juice trickled down her neck. Lee refilled the glass twice before enough reached its target.

Jesse returned their call and listened to Liu's description of Jasirey's symptoms. "Possibly a hormonal reaction," he said. "That and a brain starved of glucose could certainly cause fainting. Have Jasirey test her blood periodically and eat smaller, more frequent meals.

"On a personal note, I spoke to my wife. We can visit this weekend if convenient. I'll examine Jasirey while there."

Liu thanked him and handed the phone to Lee to arrange travel for the doctor and his wife.

"Baby, talk to me."

Jasirey squinted at Ian. "Time to get up?"

Liu fetched Jasirey's herbal drink and touched her face to focus her. "Drink this, darling."

She peered at him blankly, drank, and plucked at her nightshirt. It lifted with a sound like pulling a boot out of mud. "What's this?" She flapped the sodden shirt.

"Your blood sugar dropped," Liu said. "You required juice to level it. I spilled a bit."

Lee cradled her hand. Jasirey leaned forward to hug him and stopped. "I'm all wet." He buried his face in her neck. "It's okay, my Lee." He kissed her, feather light. "I won't break."

"No worries." His lips molded hers with certainty.

"Fael?" She held his trembling body close. "Poor Fael, I'm sorry I scared you."

"Shush, loved one. All is well. You are fine."

The next day, Liu consulted with the husbands in his office. "Until assured Jasirey's symptoms are under control, I prefer one of us stay nearby or monitor her on the intercom. Along with the obvious physical interventions, ancient lore on Jasirey suggests endorphins from sex help combat hormonal side effects." His fellow husbands' avid expressions amused him.

Having no morning meetings scheduled, Ian opted for the first shift. He woke Jasirey with soft lips and exploring hands. She stretched like a kitten being petted. He palmed one heavy breast, applied his cunning mouth to the other, and brought her to orgasm.

Jasirey purred. "Good morning to me."

Ian pulled her up, pointed her toward the bathroom, and microwaved oatmeal mixed with milk. He heaped on blueberries and walnuts and carried the breakfast tray to the bed.

Returning, Jasirey glanced at it in surprise. "I figured you had other ideas."

"Orgasm, then breakfast, the morning routine of champions."

"Nut. And your orgasm?" He spooned a bite into her mouth, so she moved on. "Afraid I haven't planned anything special for Jesse's visit to ensnare him in Jasirey's spell."

"I suspect he's already snared. Why else come to the boondocks?" When Jasirey looked away, he said, "Baby, you know I'm teasing. I love our home."

"You guys talk about the changes I've had to make. You have, too." She studied him and, satisfied he meant what he said, she smiled. "As far as Jesse goes, don't underestimate curiosity."

"My money's on you, my powerful Jasirey."

❧ ❧ ❧

After Ian left for work, Everett, who had acquired a blood glucose meter and accompanying supplies, taught Jasirey to use them. She munched on cheese and grapes as he explained the simple procedure for drawing blood. The needle hovered over her finger. She inhaled, pushed the button, and breathed. Piece of cake and normal blood sugar.

Fael joined them to invite Jasirey to explore the vegetable gardens. The day felt like a preview of summer. She wore a teal island dress made specifically for her with a fitted waist beaded in Jasirey's colors of blue, purple, and green that to her delight expanded to accommodate her growing waistline. She applied sunblock, grabbed sunglasses and a hat, and was surprised to find Fael waiting next to a car. They drove past fields of ending spring and sprouting summer vegetables as well as orchards of apple, plum, and peach trees just beginning to set fruit—a full-blown farm.

"I had no idea of the scope of Ian's plans."

Fael grinned. "Neither did he. Lee and I studied husbandry."

The final stop showed her a solar array that provided their power.

Jasirey plotted on coaxing Ian into eventually exchanging their vehicles
for electric ones.

The couple returned to the house for lunch and Jasirey's nap.
After her morning escapades, she briefly considered objecting to being
awakened by the constant barrage of Fael's lapping, nipping mouth, but
her mind misted.

Jasirey realized all the attention resulted from the previous night's
scare. She was having a really good time comforting her men.

They omitted telling her that endorphins were part of her medical
prescription. It lacked romance.

❊ ❊ ❊

In the late afternoon, instead of bringing a snack to Jasirey's craft
room where she usually saw the boys after school, Lee prepared fruit,
veggies, and dip in the adults' bedroom so Jasirey would rest while
visiting with her sons.

Christopher and Michael bounded in and pounced on the food.
They planned to have Bazir, Kirani, and two friends from town who
often jammed together, spend a long weekend as an end-of-school treat.

The teens asked to have supper in the common room. It sounded
like fun, and Jasirey had no objection. The boys shortly ran off to inform
Everett of the change in dinner plans and no doubt cajole for their
favorite junk food. Jasirey trusted Everett to sneak in something healthy.

The next day, Jasirey commandeered Kharia to go into town after
lunch and help her find a welcome gift for Jesse and his wife. She
suspected Ian insisted on four security people in order to foist a roomier
SUV on her. Kharia's head scarf surprised Jasirey.

"I feel no need for the hijab with the people. In public, men stare."
Kharia giggled. "They still stare, but now they look at the symbol of my
faith rather than my face."

"Some see it as a symbol of women's oppression rather than faith."

"Extremists sometimes make it so. For most of us, it is a symbol of
respect for Allah, our families, and if married, our husbands. My parents
came to the island from Turkey. The hijab was at one time legally
forbidden in public jobs—universities, medical offices, and such. More
than half of Islamic women in Turkey wear them in the private sector.
Forbidding it raised questions about the freedom of religion there."

50

"I understand your point and others' fears that these beliefs may be forced on women. Saudi Arabian society has only recently taken steps to alleviate placing women in the position of being legal minors. A male relative's permission was needed for anything they wanted to do. Women and men are still strictly segregated in public. The laws made it difficult for a woman to pursue a career."

Kharia averted her eyes. "I am not Saudi, nor is Turkey."

"Kharia, I'm sorry. Guess I'm not as immune to ignorance and prejudice as I hoped. I know better than to lump peoples and countries together because of certain similarities."

"Yes, as some Muslims consider all Christians to be Western devils."

Ouch. Even after her blunder, Jasirey couldn't help her curiosity. "Is Robin Christian?"

"Robin's mother, a single parent you call it, lives in Northern Ireland. He follows her Protestant Christianity. Neither of us wished to convert, and our parents struggled with our marriage. We teach our children both Islam and Christianity."

Jasirey laid a hand on her own abdomen. "Has that worked out?"

Kharia's face lit up. "Robin tells them how fortunate they are to have multiple paths to God and sees Allah's blessing in allowing us to serve our most precious lady, for He holds you and your people in his hands."

Jasirey admired the couple's steadfastness, especially when many would consider them heretics for marrying outside their religions. She humbly acknowledged the faith her people showed in placing her and her children at the center of their lives.

❧ ❧ ❧

That evening, Jasirey wanted to walk in the garden. Lee and Ian clasped arms to scoop her up and rock her to and fro. "We should get a swing," she said. "The one on the island was nice."

The four men remained quiet as they waited for her to get to her real concern.

"You guys want to discuss discipline, structure, and stuff for the babies?" They had yet to enter the territory of parenting techniques.

Lee and Ian set her on a bench. "It's understood among the Devoted," Lee said, "that you have full authority regarding the children's upbringing, even naming them."

51

Liu's eyes sparkled at her *Are you crazy?* expression. "The children learn the wisdom and skills they require from your unique attributes."

Fael kissed her forehead. "I have every confidence you intend to expose the children to the people's cultures and faiths and to support each child's chosen life path."

Jasirey doubted they'd be that nonchalant if one of their kids chose to follow beliefs foreign to theirs but merely said, "Kids need all their parents."

"Yes, we provide the male role model, point of view, love, and acceptance for balance." The perfect opening, the others' slight nods encouraged Fael. "Loved one, speaking of our role, we wished to discuss Christopher and Michael's responsibilities and self-discipline."

Jasirey's eyes flashed. Fael watched her struggle not to give in to defensiveness. His eyes assumed a mellow golden hue. "Children on the island, especially in their teenaged years, begin responsibilities as members of the Devoted and to develop whatever specific talents they may be inclined toward. Do you not think the boys ready for greater responsibility?"

"My sons inherited ADD from Roger, attention problems without hyperactivity. They're turtles. Takes them twice as long to complete tasks. Organizing and prioritizing are torture to them, the reason they hated school. I suppose I gave them too much leeway, finished or did chores myself to get them done. Poor parenting."

Lee cradled her. "Not even you can bad-mouth my wife. You are a wonderful mother."

"It is unreasonable to expect perfection from yourself," Fael said, "in either knowledge or deed. Training may assist your sons."

"What training? Where?"

Liu laid a calming hand on her stomach.

"Beginning here with us," Ian said, "and eventually on the island, whenever you and the boys decide they're ready."

"Have you any objections," Fael asked, "to us assigning the boys responsibilities and guiding them toward attaining discipline?"

Jasirey admired the neat way they'd boxed her in. Roger had been more than happy to leave the parenting to her. "They aren't motivated self-starters. I trust you to be patient. Fair warning. You're approaching this from the perspective of trainers. Whether they recognize it or not, the boys see you as father figures. Different dynamic. They want to please you but will still play the you're-not-my-father card and resent your interference."

Bugs arrived and drove them inside. Unsettled, Jasirey decided to listen to music in the living room. Lee put on the piano concertos she favored and drew her into a dance. His height and bulk never interfered with his effortless guidance of her body.

Everett rolled in a snack cart, and the men prodded him to take a spin. Ignoring their jeers, he politely declined.

Ian's lips twitched. "All right, gentlemen. He's probably tired from a long day."

Everett sniffed, approached Jasirey, and unfurled his hand. "May I?" He basked in the affectionate smile she reserved especially for him.

He steered Jasirey in wide circles like a storybook princess. When the music ended, he bowed. She briefly considered a curtsy but preferred a hug, as did he.

❧ ❧ ❧

Ian picked up Jesse and his wife, Lill, at their town airport and drove them to their new home. Jasirey felt an instant connection to the athletically built, dark-blond woman. The couple handed her a bunch of daisies, pink lilies, and lavender. She presented a gift to a surprised Lill.

"Oh, my favorite flower." She showed Jesse the silk wall hanging embroidered in lilacs.

"Daffodils and lilacs are my favorites," Jasirey said. "I hoped you'd like it."

In the early afternoon, the adults walked the grounds of the family compound. They continued outside the walls and came to the construction site of the duplex for Kharia and Robin and the teacher. The people halted work to greet them. Clear to Jesse and Lill, they aimed their bows at Jasirey. A man approached carrying a basket.

"We found the strawberries growing wild on the property and intended to deliver them for your dinner. They have a richer flavor than the cultivated variety. I fashioned the basket from reeds back on the island, a gift for our lady."

Hormone-heightened sentiment brought tears to Jasirey's eyes. She buried her face in Lee's neck as he lifted her despite her weak protest. The people dispersed in understanding when Liu suggested returning to the house and a nap for Jasirey.

Fael led Jesse and Lill into the living room to relate the unclassified history of the Devoted.

Ian explained Jasirey's mission and the role of her children but not the prophecy and second pregnancy.

Fascinated by the story, Jesse and Lill nonetheless felt out of their element.

Liu's eyes held sympathy. "Let us meet whenever you wish at the pool. Everett shall show you its location and your room."

Jesse and Lill stammered their thanks.

For the first time, Fael and Liu clearly understood Jasirey's concerns regarding others' acceptance. Everett's reaction they'd dismissed as a natural bias for Ian. Having never spoken of the Devoted to anyone not searching for a new life purpose, the men could only imagine the stronger negative response less professional, less invested people than Jesse and Lill might have.

❧ ❧ ❧

Alone with Lill in the lovely guestroom decorated in shades of blue, Jesse said, "Unreal."

"If it were just her and the men," Lill said, "you could discount it."

"Might be a cult." Jesse considered a moment. "I got no vibe anyone was coerced or brainwashed. Those people seemed genuinely fond of her."

"And the husbands obviously adore her, but it seems an awful lot to place on her."

"She can handle it."

Lill studied him.

Flushing, he rubbed her arms. "Just an impression. Wish I hadn't brought you?"

"Hell, no. This is the most interesting thing I've encountered in a long time."

Jesse fingered Lill's chin-length bob. "Excepting me, I hope."

She rolled her eyes. "Sexual energy permeates the air here like humidity."

He coaxed her closer. "I have eyes only for you, my love."

"Uh-huh, and you aren't the least bit attracted to Jasirey."

"Uh-huh, and you only stared at Lee's dreadlocks."

In the late afternoon, the adults sat by the pool at a folding table covered by a flowery tablecloth. Jasirey's stomach rumbled at platters of sandwiches, cut vegetables, and apple-date cake, not that she could digest the cake anymore. "You look rested," she said to Lill, who hid her blush in a sandwich.

Six teenagers crashed into the room, abruptly halted, then walked sedately to the table.

Jasirey introduced them and offered a snack, which they consumed with assembly-line rapidity. She sighed at the demolished cake, mentally shrugged, and chatted with Lill while the guys played volleyball, teens against the adults.

"This is a lovely house," Lill said.

Jasirey smiled. "I had fun helping to plan it."

"I'll admit my curiosity at Jesse's description of your family. Your . . . husbands explained the Devoted and your role. Your sons are cuties."

Jasirey grinned. "I won't disagree. Kirani and Bazir's parents are members of the Devoted. The other boys live in town. We tell outsiders that Liu, Lee, and Fael handle the farm and security."

Lill understood Jasirey's implied reminder of their confidentiality agreement plus a direct invitation to become part of the inner circle. Not sure why it pleased her, she thought of Jasirey as an average woman. Well, except for the glorious smile that pulled you in, conveyed caring and, somehow, peacefulness.

From her thankfully short bout of severe queasiness during her first pregnancy, Lill recognized Jasirey's effort to hide her discomfort. "Jesse says you've been pretty ill. Please don't feel obligated to entertain me."

"I'm usually the first one in the pool. Not today. Thanks for the concern. Many would consider me stupid for getting pregnant at my age, me included till the ultrasound." She watched the shouting, taunting volleyball players for a moment. "Everything happened so fast. Becoming Jasirey, marrying my husbands. Seems longer than four months."

"Really? I assumed you'd been together a good deal longer."

"Assimilating being Jasirey is the harder part. My husbands and I bonded right away. They're extraordinary guys and husbands."

Divided over what she believed about the Devoted, Lill concentrated on Jasirey. "Jesse says you want our families to be friends. I'd like that, too."

"Thank you, Lill. I've been able to tell so few people about my new life. That means a lot to me."

❧ ❧ ❧

Six teens and ten adults vied to be heard at the dining-room table. Kharia apologized to the visitors. "Our house will soon be finished and allow some peace at Jasirey's dinners."

On her other side, Jesse thought Jasirey looked pale. "Are you all right?"

"It's the noise. We'll send the boys upstairs in a bit."

In the living room with after-dinner beverages, Lill asked Kharia what prompted the couple to move to America.

"Our boys became friends. Jasirey requested our assistance, and we wished to serve."

Robin leaned forward. "We waited a considerable time for our lady to be revealed. Jasirey has power and caring, born to lead. We wanted a part in her mission."

Unaware of any formal political affiliations, Jesse asked, "What type of power?"

"You cannot be near her long and resist a pull at your heart. She feels another's pain and helps or encourages, changes lives for the better. It's a considerable honor to serve her."

The summation confused Jasirey. When had she done any of that?

Like a small boy with a tenuous hold on a secret, Robin grinned. "Jasirey's humbleness also endears her to us. Doesn't realize her true impact, does she. Many on the island tell of how she influenced their lives directly or in the smaller ripples fanning out from the larger."

Her head throbbing painfully, Jasirey stood on wobbly legs.

Liu noticed Jesse trying to catch his attention. Seeing Jasirey's face, he hastily rose to escort her upstairs.

In the elevator, the two men grabbed hold as she lurched forward, vomited, and mortified at the mess, began to cry.

On the bed, Jesse fitted the blood pressure cuff but had to wait as Jasirey suffered a second bout of illness.

"Blood pressure's slightly elevated," he said in his calm doctor's tone.

Liu removed his wife's soiled dress to place acupuncture needles. When the pain and nausea abated, Liu took her to the bathroom and washed her legs where vomit had splashed up.

Grateful for his steady presence, Jasirey leaned on him a moment. Liu returned her to bed and propped her on pillows in case of further upheaval.

He consulted Jesse in the sitting area.

"Her blood pressure returned to normal after the acupuncture," Jesse said quietly. "I assume you know the signs of preeclampsia."

Liu nodded. A precursor to eclampsia and its possible seizures, coma, and death, preeclampsia's symptoms included high blood pressure, swelling of the extremities, and protein in the urine.

"The goal is to prevent vomiting, preferably without drugs, and promote controlled weight gain," Jesse said. "If Jasirey recognizes distress prior to the point of illness, you may have time to stop it."

They decided to speak to her about it in the morning.

Ian, Fael, and Lee entertained their guests awhile longer before joining Liu to discuss Robin's unprecedented insight into their wife's abilities. It brought home something they'd lost sight of as they dealt with her physical problems. As husband-protectors, they carried responsibility for encouraging Jasirey to fulfill her duties and simultaneously to prevent her obligations from becoming onerous, a tightrope act. None of the men slept well.

Jasirey woke earlier than usual with a vague headache and a rumbling stomach, which erased sex from the morning routine.

Jesse came in and suggested she learn the triggers for her nausea and inform Liu at the first sign, so he might prevent vomiting.

Irritation also followed Jasirey out of sleep. Nearly snapping that, of course, she'd say if she knew she'd be sick, she realized the problem lay with her and bit it back as she tried to concentrate. Her headache worsened. She gained a certain satisfaction in informing Liu.

The rest of the family, Jesse, and Lill gathered for breakfast before attending a prayer service for Jasirey held by the Devoted who worked at the compound.

Jesse and Lill enjoyed stories and songs of legendary Jasireys and the current bearer of the name. The couple concluded that, clearly part of a centuries-old culture rather than fanatically opinionated, the Devoted celebrated various beliefs and united in one purpose—to serve their lady and her children. They prayed to a supreme power, not Jasirey, in joyful, optimistic thankfulness.

Liu called Everett midmorning and asked for something he hoped might perk up Jasirey's appetite.

Emerging from the shower, she found scrambled eggs with vegetables and cheese, blueberries, and peanut-buttered toast waiting on the table. She made a face but ate a slice of toast and a few bites of eggs and berries.

After ensuring that breakfast settled, Liu and Jasirey went to the garden to sit on the newly acquired swing while waiting for the others.

The day became quite warm. Jasirey suspected that when summer's heat arrived in earnest, she'd be housebound. She thanked God and Ian for the pool, apt to be her summer retreat.

When the group returned, Jasirey asked, "Will you be my doctor and our friend, Jesse?"

"I will." Tension eased from her shoulders, and Jesse was touched that she wanted his acceptance.

She thanked him and asked them to visit again.

Jesse laughed. "That's not power just plain old manipulation. Get me to come here and save you the trip."

"Did it work?" Jasirey's imp peeked out.

"This time." Lill had told him she would enjoy another visit. "We'll schedule something in a few weeks depending on your condition." He raised a warning finger. "The appointment after that, you're required at the office for tests."

Jesse squatted in front of Jasirey. "Expect those babies to grow rapidly now. Don't be stubborn. Rest whenever possible. Once they arrive, the opportunity to be pampered disappears."

❧ ❧ ❧

The end of June brought record-breaking humid weather. Jasirey's discomfort rose with the heat, the searing temperature outside mirroring the burning acid reflux clawing her insides. A blander diet and sleeping propped on pillows alleviated it somewhat but did not eliminate the symptoms. Jasirey began to despise food and sometimes retched on pure bile.

Despite her tears, Liu put his foot down and scheduled small meals every two hours. He told her to consider it practice for the babies' feeding schedule.

She stuck her tongue out at him.

The day prior to the Fourth of July, a cold front arrived. Sky-wide flashes, bone-jarring cracks, and grumbling echoes rivaled any fireworks display. The holiday temperature reached the eighties, though not terribly humid.

The people enjoyed the spirit of the American celebration. They built firepits to cook hamburgers, hot dogs, fish, chicken, and roasted vegetables. At the end of the evening, everyone watched in wonderment as a crew hired by Ian set off fireworks. Bright white, loud flash-bulb pops overlaid scintillating blooms of red, blue, gold, and green.

Jasirey stayed indoors during the sunlight hours but ventured outside for the fireworks. Burnt gunpowder wafting through the night sky and the explosive assault on her eardrums drove her back to the house. Liu accompanied her, but she insisted that he return to the party.

Deeming it best not to upset his mulish wife, he turned on the intercom, leaving Everett to monitor her.

More and more frequently, the horrid sensation of ants crawling on her legs, arms, abdomen, even her face made Jasirey want to scream. She slapped at the intercom. They should leave her alone. She paced on the verge of running, her breath rasping. Sweat dampened her nightshirt. It clung, and in a fury, she twisted to grab at the saturated hem.

Fael disliked leaving their wife in the company of nothing save the intercom. The turkey frank he had eaten congealed in his gut. Halfway through the fireworks, he gave in to the compulsion to check on her and sprinted toward the house.

The bed lay empty. Fael turned to the bathroom.

"Loved one!"

He skidded to his knees beside her body sprawled on the floor and deftly searched her for injuries. He flipped on the intercom and urged Everett to call Liu. Half dragging, half carrying, he set Jasirey on the bed. He fumbled the first strip in the glucose meter and then cursed himself for having to prick her again.

Everett rushed in and took over. The meter read on the low side, not dangerous.

The others pounded up the stairs, and Fael recounted how he'd found her.

Everett's body stilled and drooped as he berated himself for not hearing her fall.

Liu attempted to remove her sodden, resistant nightshirt.

Lee tore it in half, and Fael joined him to rub Jasirey's extremities, her skin cold and pale as moonlight.

Ian called Jesse and relayed Liu's findings—pupils responded normally, heart and lungs sounded fine. He heard strong fetal heartbeats.

"That soaked and no vomit," Jesse said. "Find out what she was doing."

Fael informed them of the turned-off intercom. They let that go for the moment.

"She's coming to," Lee said.

Liu's thumb gently stroked Jasirey's cheek. "Darling, wake now."

"Go 'way."

The men smiled at one another. Ian cradled her to his chest while Liu held the phone for Jesse to speak to her.

Sharp and clipped, he said, "You terrified your husbands. What were you doing?"

"Don't know. Couldn't stand it."

"Jasirey, couldn't stand what?"

"The ants—crawling—kept crawling." Tears shimmered on her lashes. "Had to stop . . ."

"All right, sweetheart. It'll be all right." He spoke to Liu. "I think she was in physical distress and overexerted. She doesn't appear to be in danger. Give her that drink of yours and check her glucose level often to be on the safe side. And Liu? Don't scold her. I doubt she was able to make rational decisions at the time."

Liu thanked Jesse and repeated his advice to the others.

"Poor little mite." Everett kissed her head. "I am sorry I missed this."

"Not your fault," Ian said. He closed his eyes and caressed Jasirey's hair with his chin.

A rare occurrence, Jasirey woke at first light. She remembered little of the night before except for her husbands' acute distress.

Guilt reared. Even sleeping, they looked unrested, haggard. Careful not to wake them, Jasirey brought an apple and a hard-boiled egg with her to Ian's office where she could contact Kai. She hoped the time difference worked out. Her ability to concentrate and analyze had deserted her in recent days.

The morning's work pleased Jasirey. She asked Everett to carry a tray of cinnamon rolls, cantaloupe, and eggs with broccoli and cheese back to the bedroom. Jasirey kissed his cheek in thanks before debating the best way to wake her men.

She chose soft and warm. Someone laid a sleepy hand on her bottom. "Breakfast," she said firmly and beckoned them to the dining nook.

Liu studied her coloring. "How long have you been awake?"

"Not long. I'm hungry." The men watched her eat a sizeable breakfast. It required substantial effort for her to play the charade. Wrung-out but resolved to spare them further worry, Jasirey forced down the last bite of a cinnamon roll she'd likely regret. "I heard some of the people hope to return to the island for the summer."

"Since building has slowed, a number wish to," Lee said. "We'll handle the details."

"Bazir and Kirani plan to visit their grandmother. My boys asked to be included. I thought you guys might accompany them and consult Kai on starting appropriate training."

"Is that what you thought?" Ian said coolly.

Damn. "Just for a week during Jesse and Lill's visit."

As the doctor and his wife planned to stay only for two days, Liu dismissed that.

"Everett will be here." *Poor Everett.* Jasirey hated to burden him.

"It does not require four men to care for two boys," Fael said.

Ian flared. "She's angling for something entirely different, ordering us to the island."

Jasirey's eyes fired back. "I'm not asking you to desert me, for God's sake. I'm saying my men look like hell. Take a break from the tension and the pressure. Go, meditate, talk to Kai—anything to erase that weariness from your wonderful faces." She radiated love. "Since Jesse said my stamina will deteriorate as they grow, this is probably your last chance before the babies arrive and for who knows how long after. Return to me restored and rejuvenated. Please."

Ian rubbed his forehead. She always managed to expertly deflate him. He plucked her from her chair and rested his head on her breast. "What can I do with such a woman except love her back? Though warming your backside's still an option."

Jasirey kissed his smooth head. "Yeah, yeah. Say you'll go."

"Difficult, stubborn woman. What do you think?" he asked the men.

Jasirey kissed Liu's troubled eyes. "Please go."

"I first wish to speak to Jesse."

"Already done. He said, quote, 'You won't do your wife any good if you're stressed out. We'll try to arrange a long weekend and take care of her for you.' End quote."

Lee bristled. "You've been plotting behind our backs."

"Only since this morning. Kai says to think of it as a power nap."

Fael settled her on his lap. "You have been busy, and this activity has exacted its toll. You feel unwell. What shall we do with you?"

She admitted to not being one hundred percent. "All the stress watching out for my men."

He didn't laugh.

Jasirey twined about his neck. "Kiss me and make it all better."

Wet, warm mouths explored, fingers glided over skin, and hard and soft met gently in an achingly good, drawn-out pleasure that left them all full of endorphins and feeling better.

❧ ❧ ❧

The final days prior to departure, Jasirey struggled against irritation at her solicitous husbands. By Thursday, when Jesse and Lill arrived for dinner, she had convinced herself it would be a relief to have them gone. Friday morning, she hugged and kissed the four teens. Fear of dissolving into a pathetic puddle prevented her from admitting she'd miss her husbands.

The men managed good-humored farewells, though their worries leaked out in extended hugs.

After the large group left for the airport, Jesse steered the women into the living room. "Flood time," he said to Jasirey.

She pressed her face into his chest, whimpered, and hated the sound. "I'm out of whack."

"Yes, you are, but as a very pregnant woman, you're entitled to a few tears."

"Every day, every few hours?"

He patted her face. "We'll only worry if you become dehydrated."

The Men Take Stock

Master Kai and relatives of the returning people gathered at
the island airstrip to greet the plane. Jasirey had seen correctly. Her
husbands did indeed appear more worn than the trip alone warranted.
Master Kai gave thanks for her wisdom in sending them.

Bazir and Kirani's grandmother and sister met them. Christopher felt
a zinging thrum along his spine. He had never noticed Zubeena's long
eyelashes before. He turned beet red when she kissed his cheeks in welcome.

The stepfathers led the way to the training center dormitory. They
bunked in one room, Michael and Christopher sharing with a couple of
security trainees. They stored their luggage and wandered the island. People
continually hailed them, Jasirey's health and pregnancy the sole topic.

The boys steeled themselves for more of the same at the Imperiat
domicile where the family had been invited to dinner. Instead, the
Imperiat concentrated on them.

Asked, the teens agreed they felt ambivalent about the unseen
babies and worried for their mom. They could talk to their stepfathers,
who loved their mother and yes, probably them, too. Vague musings
comprised their hopes for the future.

"Your mother wishes that you be shown the training opportunities
here," Master Kai said. "A meeting has been scheduled for the morning."

Michael chewed his nails.

"Pinpointing areas of interest will suffice for this week, yes?"

Michael nodded vigorously.

After they all finished the meal, Master Kai winked at the teens.
"Do you prefer to return to the training center while we speak to your
stepfathers regarding your mother's health?"

They gratefully opted to go.

Master Kai regarded the men. Fael and Lee straightened, Liu stared
at the table. Ian's fingers continually skimmed his head. "Our lady

contacted me, concerned for your welfare. I heard no complaint or lack of confidence in you, simply worry for her husbands."

Another Imperiat said, "We, however, detect a woeful lack of energy. We expressed our grave concern that four are inadequate for the task you have undertaken. Pitfalls must be expected. Yet the responsibility for Jasirey's care rests on you."

"Let us take this week," Master Kai said, "to assess your abilities and weaknesses, address your concerns and fears, and strategize ways to strengthen you."

"Go rest, gentlemen," a woman said. "Plans are in place for the care of Christopher and Michael. We shall begin in the morning."

❧ ❧ ❧

Jasirey woke early, chilled without her men's warm bodies surrounding her. Her heart ached in a weird mind-body way. She missed the cuddling, good morning kisses, twining limbs, soft curves yielding to hard strength. *Okay, stop. Breathe.* She climbed out of the bed.

Everett's voice filled the room. He refused to allow anyone else to monitor her. "Good morning, my dear. Did you sleep well?"

Her voice sang out. "Better than you, I bet." *Poor Everett.* She couldn't remember how many times she'd risen to pace or use the bathroom. She rubbed her chest. It felt hollow, and even though she knew better, Jasirey continually strained to hear a footstep or a masculine murmur. She understood why the council warned that Jasirey and her husbands' emotional and physical bonds were equally crucial to their well-being.

"The doctor requests that you meet him in Liu's office at nine o'clock."

"I'll be ready for breakfast in an hour. I want to soak in the tub, warm up a little."

"Are you ill?" Panic laced his voice.

"No, just used to more body heat."

"Ah, of course," he mumbled. "An hour, but first drink a glass of milk, please, to ensure your blood sugar remains stable."

Jasirey ran a bath and found a box of rarely used bath salts pushed to the back of the sink cabinet. Lavender was supposed to be soothing. She folded a thick towel for her head and slipped in. Heat enveloped her, caused a hard shiver, and slowly seeped in. Jasirey willed her body to relax. Her mind drifted into daydreams that inevitably evolved into erotic fantasies. Funny—her sole recourse for a healthy libido in the marriage to Roger, masturbation hadn't entered her mind since she met Ian.

Hands roamed a body no longer familiar to her. At only four months, her breasts and belly were huge. *Don't dwell on it,* she admonished herself. *Think of your men's bodies. Ian, all planes and angles, forever threatening to spank her. Pleasure from being hit—it must be something sensual, not a real blow.* She'd flatten anyone who deliberately hurt her. *Okay, off track and not setting the mood.*

Fantasy—draped over the back of a sofa wearing a short T-shirt that barely covered her non-pregnant and perfectly toned bottom, Ian standing naked and fully aroused to the side, an image that kick started her pulse. She imagined his large hand running from her ankle to her hip. She knew it would tickle, and her back arched in anticipation.

"You like that?" Ian whispered in her head. "Want more?"

Jasirey's finger glided between her legs in the bath as she pictured Ian kneading her bottom to pull on her pleasure core. After eliciting several moans, he slid in two fingers.

"Squeeze," his voice purred, lifting the hairs on her neck. "Squeeze tighter, or I'll spank you." His breathing roughened. "I want to spank you. Force your muscles to clench hard around me."

As he had so many actual times, Ian rotated his fingers while his other hand skimmed her bottom, skin against skin. "Tighter," he whispered in her ear. His hand lifted and smacked down.

In the bath, Jasirey's muscles clenched with a literal bolt of pleasure. The glide of his hand—the lift—slap—and again, skin to warming skin.

"I want you to squeeze me, baby."

Jasirey shuddered in the lavender-laced hot water. Deep into the fantasy, she felt his fingers leaving her before he sheathed his body in hers, withdrew slowly, and buried himself, hands molding her bottom.

"Come on, baby." His teeth gritted. "Tighter." A hand lifted and landed.

Jasirey's finger circled faster and pressed harder.

"Again." The lift of his fantasy hand, the slap, body surging, lift, slap.

Jasirey's body bowed in an explosive release and slowly melted into the tub as she acclimated to her own body.

Wow. Such intensity when alone was a first.

Laughing to herself—at herself—Jasirey hazily pondered asking Ian whether the reality of spanking had any resemblance to her fantasy. Picturing his possible reaction, she shivered.

Her body hummed and her mind emptied, drifting until the water cooled and she roused herself.

Breakfast waited on the table. "Hey, pancakes. Trying to spoil me, Everett?"

He used almond flour, easier to digest and a healthier alternative for gaining weight. He audibly sniffed, and she laughed.

"Eat, young lady."

"Thanks, Everett. I really appreciate you going above and beyond. After the guys get home, you should visit your family since they can't come here this year."

Everett had told her they usually visited each year but knew nothing of the Devoted.

"Perhaps later. Let us first concentrate on getting you safely through this pregnancy."

"I love you, you know."

"Yes, my dear, and I, you."

❧ ❧ ❧

Liu had transformed his office into an exam room. Jesse patted the table. "Up you go." He examined her. "Babies have grown well. You should feel movement soon."

"It may be hard to tell the difference between baby-fluttering and ant-crawling."

"I'm hoping that eases as the pregnancy progresses."

The rest of the morning, Jasirey, Jesse, and Lill lounged around the pool. Everett provided the requisite snack. Jasirey managed her queasy stomach past lunch and, fighting to keep the meal down, spent the afternoon lying on her left side in the living room at Jesse and Lill's insistence. She drew slow, deep breaths as sweat glistened on her forehead.

"Guys, this is no fun for you. I'm going upstairs."

"Okay," Jesse said. Lill pulled at his sleeve and shook her head. He patted her hand.

67

Jasirey swung her legs to the floor and lifted her head. Groaning, she fell back.

Jesse wiped her damp forehead. "Going to behave?"

She glared feebly and threw up into a trash can. Midafternoon, she slept.

"God, Jesse." Lill kept her voice low. "How do the men do this day in and day out? We haven't done much, but the stress of watching her suffer, I'm exhausted."

"Me, too, babe." He rubbed her tense shoulders. "Is it odd, do you think, this rapid friendship? We hardly know them."

"Now that you mention it." Her gaze on Jasirey softened. "They seem like family."

Everett carried in Jasirey's drink. Jesse frowned. "She hasn't slept long."

"I've seen her husbands hold her in these circumstances and place the straw in her mouth. Though not truly awake, she drinks."

"All right, we'll try it." Jesse lifted Jasirey for Lill to shove cushions under her.

Everett laid the straw on her mouth. She attempted to roll away, so Jesse petted her hair, calling her name. His mouth twisted after several attempts to get her to drink.

"Her husbands make it look easier," Everett said.

Lill worried her lower lip. "Maybe we could skip this snack."

"Let's test her." Jessie had Everett ask one of the people to fetch the meter and pricked Jasirey's finger. "It's mid-range but I have no idea how precipitately it drops." He weighed his knowledge of her condition and symptoms. "I prefer not to chance it."

Jasirey's head on his chest, Jesse held the glass, poured in a small amount, and stroked her throat until she swallowed. He eased the straw into her mouth. They all sighed in relief as she drank it and finished two-thirds. He decided that would do and set Jasirey on the pillows.

Lill hugged Jesse for herself as well as him. "Good job, honey."

"No wonder she sent the men off. Even with four of them, they no doubt needed the break. Does this happen often?"

"Too often," Everett said. "The nausea and the debilitating effects of everything together. At first, I couldn't imagine one woman and four husbands. Now I believe the stories of past Jasireys having far more."

"Poor husbands," a sleepy-eyed Jasirey said. "It might be better for them, but I couldn't handle extra men. There are only so many orifices."

Lill, Jesse, and Everett stared, speechless. Lill's hand flew to her mouth. Too late. The laugh burst into the room. Jesse brayed.

"Really," Everett muttered.

Lit up in impish delight, Jasirey said, "Sorry, Everett."

To his mind, she was not the least repentant.

Jesse thought Jasirey's swift return to consciousness proved the necessity of them persevering with her smoothie. She ate a decent dinner. Afterwards, they played cards. Despite her resiliency, he insisted on a short evening and, with Lill, walked Jasirey to her room.

"Sorry again for the pain I've been."

Jesse kissed her forehead. "I'm sure your men consider you worth every minute of effort. So do we."

Jasirey's radiant smile and affectionate hug helped to erase the afternoon's ordeal.

❧ ❧ ❧

The island's restorative herbal drink eased Michael and Christopher through the time difference. Mornings, Elders led tours of training classes. Computer applications topped the list for future pursuit. Afternoons, they enjoyed martial-arts lessons in the company of Kirani and Bazir capped off with a visit to the pond. Christopher considered asking why Zubeena didn't come along but felt weird. They saw their stepfathers only at dinner.

The teens learned a great deal about Jasirey from their roommates, trainees not much older than the boys. Their mother's heroics at the Imperiatu shocked them. Their hearts swelled with pride at the trainees' admiration of her strength and courage. Her prophecy floored them. *Quadruplets now and quintuplets later? Holy shit.*

For their better understanding of the Devoted, a nice woman named Amador explained recruiting, not a job they were allowed to do as children of Jasirey but important to the history of the Devoted. Recruiters searched for people with physical skills or gifted in traits such as wisdom who might be helpful to Jasirey. They had searched for Jasirey herself before they found their mother.

"Now that we have our Jasirey," Amador said, "recruiting shall slow down until more people are needed to aid her children. I returned to the island to teach new recruiters. I find myself drawn, however, more toward learning the best practices for farming in arid conditions with the goal to allow people to survive in their own countries."

The teens' eyes glazed over as Amador recited things she'd learned. She patted their shoulders. "I suspect farming is not in your futures. What would you like to learn about?"

"Missions," both teens said.

Amador recited the G-rated story of her mission with their stepfathers in the Central African Republic where they had rescued kidnapped children. Christopher and Michael couldn't wait to ask the trainees they bunked with what they knew of their stepfathers as a mission team. The men had been holding out on them.

❋ ❋ ❋

Ian, Liu, Lee, and Fael rose in the predawn hours to exercise for an hour and meditate. They arrived at the Imperiat domicile at sunrise to spend the day fasting and delving into thoughts and feelings they had left unexplored.

As did all the husbands, Ian battled guilt at impregnating his cherished wife while not considering what she alone must suffer. Plus, he had brought her to the island yet hadn't resolved the resentment he harbored at being married to Jasirey rather than Shannon. He loved his core family. Liu's words concerning other lovers and the Imperiat's proclamation that Protectors would father the next pregnancy gnawed at his gut.

The Imperiat chipped at Ian's resistance and encouraged him to acknowledge his rage at the mere notion of any man save her husbands having access to her heart. Ian knew that, not geared for casual sex, Jasirey would not give herself to anyone she did not love.

The Imperiat guided Ian toward accepting feelings as unavoidable and understanding that actions determined their positive or negative impact. Festering resentment led to negative actions that could erode the foundation of love. To thrive, love though an emotion required positive actions leading to positive thoughts. Ian adopted the words do love—pun intended to keep the fun in it—as his mantra. To him, actions leading to thoughts meant fake it till you make it.

Worry dragged at Liu's heart. He better understood the risks and complications of their wife's pregnancy and the toll the progressing growth might take on her not inexhaustible strength. As a Protector, he hadn't expected Jasirey to be found in his lifetime and had devoted himself to a dream of her and the practice of medicine.

Proved wrong, Liu blessed his precious one for nudging his course from a stodgy badger bachelorhood to a vibrant life of love and family. The prophecy troubled him. Jasirey's vision thus far rang true, the reality harsher than he had imagined. And her destiny beyond children had not yet started. Barely acknowledging his fears, Liu had no release valve for the anger they created.

The Imperiat realized that reminding Liu of Jasirey's divinely scripted and therefore protected mission would have little or no effect. They instead provided meditation techniques and mental exercises to switch his focus from what he could not control to concentrating on the emotional support and healthcare Jasirey needed. Throughout the week, he practiced being mindful in recognizing his fears, especially when they turned to anger, and how to transform anger into the energy he needed. Liu intended to share the exercises with the others at home.

Lee depended on his strength, skills, or good-humored appeal to manipulate circumstances to his liking and chafed at his uselessness in protecting Jasirey from illness. It sucked—one of his wife's favorite Americanisms. Lee considered pregnancy a time of inaction, at least on the father's part. Overseeing security for his family and working on the farm kept him busy. He found his disquiet mystifying.

The Imperiat left Lee to meditate without instruction. At day's end, it required a concerted effort for his muscles to lift him. The unbidden image surfaced of Jasirey often experiencing the same with her expanding girth. Reminded of their lady's indomitable will, he slept well. The second day, a glimmer of enlightenment flitted in and out of a brain too fogged to catch it. Lee missed his wife.

Determined to focus on meditation the third day, he nevertheless gave in and daydreamed of her the entire time. He enjoyed it immensely. The glimmer returned the next day in mind-boggling simplicity. The fifth day, Lee performed a series of martial art katas. The precise movements pushed his body to the limit. He thought of nothing at all.

The ultimate Protector, God chose Jasirey. The future rested in God's hands. What else could one want or require? Chosen by Jasirey, Lee belonged at his wife's side and at her service in any way possible always. The Imperiat dismissed Lee. He spent the last day on the island in the company of family and friends.

To focus on himself, Fael first had to detach from the unit the four husbands formed. Led to realize that he emotionally held back from Jasirey in a defense against her powerful psyche, he also wrestled with guilt, thus creating a barrier that impinged on his ability to be a safe place for her.

The Imperiat guided Fael to accept the fact that he did not possess Jasirey's remarkable tolerance for emotional and physical pain as not so much a failure on his part but more as a common difference between men and women. Specifically, the Imperiat encouraged Fael to accept that Jasirey's emotional and physical stamina far exceeded his.

Asked to concentrate on ways he personally contributed to the welfare of his beloved, he released any residual idolization and honestly assessed Jasirey's strengths, fears, and needs that, because of his similar gifts, he better understood. Fael gained an empowering sense of purpose. He realized that the charmer not only charms the snake, but the snake strengthens the charmer by enabling and encouraging her life's purpose.

The week away proved a wise investment. The Imperiat imparted final instructions for proceeding as a foursome of husbands and as individuals and warned of the ease with which old habits and thought patterns might tend to reassert themselves in the familiarity of home.

The husbands promised to be vigilant.

Pleased at the men's progress, the Imperiat released them.

❧ ❧ ❧

To Everett's vast relief, the family returned as scheduled. During the nightmarish week of their absence, Jasirey had stayed to herself. He worried that she hid a deteriorating condition to spare him.

In truth, Jasirey lacked the energy to constantly reassure others of her good health. Besides, she disliked lying.

On their return, the men swooped down on their wife as they lifted, hugged, and kissed her until she begged for air. Kirani and Bazir bowed and shyly hugged her. Weirdly awestruck by all the stories they'd heard, Michael and Christopher held on to their mom a little longer than usual.

Ian stopped short at sight of Everett who appeared to have aged several years. Liu and Ian guided him to the quieter kitchen where Everett described Jasirey's week.

She joined them and rested her head on Everett's shoulder. "I'm sorry you've had a rough time."

He pressed his lips to her forehead. Pushed by the men, he went to his room to rest.

"Poor Everett. I can't do this to him again." Jasirey linked her arms in Ian and Liu's. "Guess you're stuck with me." She squeezed. "You guys look better."

"I hate to admit it," Ian said, "but time on the island put our worries into perspective and renewed our energy. Thank you, love." His lips claimed hers and sent tingles straight to her toes. Liu added fuel to the fire.

Good manners prevailing, they returned to the living room. Kharia wheeled in a snack, and then she and Robin escorted their sons to their newly finished house. The stepfathers shooed the boys off to nap. Jasirey gave only a token objection to Lee carrying her upstairs as the others followed. In their room, he removed one of the island dresses she had taken to wearing every day.

He cooed as he caressed her tummy. "Let me see our babies." Kneeling to kiss the belly grown so amazingly in one week, he reared back as though punched.

Jasirey beckoned her husbands and placed their hands on the small ripples. She laughed at their fierce concentration. "They're excited their daddies are home."

Ian patted her ass to quiet her and became sidetracked. He caressed her curves and nibbled along her spine. Jasirey attempted to fondle her husbands, the men too excited to allow it. They gloried in the loving welcome glowing from those blue-green eyes: hearts, minds, and bodies giving and taking, reaffirming the bond so necessary to each of them.

As Jasirey had warned, Christopher and Michael resented their stepfathers for butting in and their mother for supporting the so-called adulthood training. What was the point of making your bed every day? They cut down on dusting by shoving things into closets. Unfortunately, the next week they had to organize those closets. Cleaning toilets was disgusting. They enjoyed Everett's cooking lessons but decided between themselves that, when on their own, they'd order take-out.

Robin introduced the four teens to molding mortar for building the compound walls and for more artistic endeavors.

Recognizing that their visit to the island was not the time to approach their stepfathers regarding missions, Michael and Christopher figured Robin provided the second best option. They, Kirani, and Bazir spent two days being gofers for artisans working on wall entrance ornaments—an eagle, wings wide spread; a bear, a ferret, and a coiled serpent—the animal spirits Jasirey saw in the men she loved and one of her abilities that, in the beginning, pointed to her being Jasirey.

Robin pointed to the snake and said, "It was a shock, true enough, to hear Jasirey declare Fael's spirit animal was a serpent when she chose him as a husband. Toad, we called him. He has wicked control over that long tongue of his."

The four teens badgered for details. Robin considered and smiled. "I've been on missions as a driver, but not so much since you bairns were born," he said at Bazir and Kirani's startled looks. To Christopher and Michael, he said, "I worked with your stepdads some, driving them on missions. Once, we escorted a mum and three daughters to a larger town where there was work and—well, where she could be home nights, and the girls could attend school. Before leaving, their uncle arrived and grabbed the littlest child, near to breaking her arm, angry at educating females, the stupid sod."

Robin cleared his throat. "Anyway, the girl shrieking, the mother begging. Fael sidles close, flicks that tongue at the man's ear and, quick as lightning, at the other. Made the man grab at both. Fael, Liu, and Ian lifted the children to the car and safely away."

Disappointed at the bland ending, Bazir said, "And what about the man, then?"

Robin's eyes twinkled. "Didn't think it wise to tangle with Lee, did he?"

Liu adjusted plans for the next appointment in Boston when Jesse mentioned that at the present point in her pregnancy, Jasirey should remain on the ground and not travel by air. Concerned about the stress of a one-day trip and preferring not to bring a cavalcade of security and housekeepers to open the small Boston house, Liu booked a hotel for two nights.

Neither Lee nor Fael had witnessed an ultrasound, but both accompanying Liu and Jasirey to Jesse's office seemed one too many. They decided to draw straws, and with Lee drawing the short straw, Fael won.

The day of the trip, Jasirey frowned at the ostentatious limo Ian provided, but after being able to stretch out and nap comfortably during the drive into Boston, she felt energetic and more appreciative on their arrival.

Fael suggested a visit to Faneuil Hall, which offered a metal-sculpture exhibit. Afterward, they found a waterfront restaurant with excellent seafood. The dessert menu tempted Jasirey despite the havoc it would wreak on her stomach. She sighed and laid the menu on the table.

Fael clasped her hand, his thumb lightly tickling her inner wrist. "Shall we save dessert for the hotel?" Molten eyes glittered.

Jasirey averted her gaze from Fael. Liu's hand caressed her knee. She glanced at her handsome men and blushed.

Bemused by her reaction, Liu said, "Anything amiss, precious one?"

She giggled. "This is weird. Reminds me of a first date or something."

"A ritual we missed." Fael trailed fingertips over her neck, shoulders, and inner arms.

Liu's hand glided from knee to thigh. Their wife possessed few non-sensitive places.

Hoping she hid her heightened breathing, Jasirey peeked at the other diners. A sizzle of recognition jolted her. Dark eyes met hers with frank appreciation—the businessman who had hit on her at the resort. He inclined his head in greeting as he passed their table and went out the door.

Strafe sat in his car for some time. Ian had married the little temptress, but Liu and Fael obviously tag-teamed her, which meant the big guy probably shared her as well. Ian had to be aware of and okay with the relationship. For what he had witnessed was a relationship, not casual sex on the side.

Lust had blazed in Fael's eyes and mellowed to tenderness at the woman's inexplicable and, Strafe bet, real shyness. Though Marcus believed she was six months along, she looked ready to pop. Under Marcus's orders, Strafe had been keeping tabs on Ian and his team since their move to the States.

By coincidence, Strafe had seen the group by Faneuil Hall and followed them to the art exhibit where he had watched Liu coax the woman to rest against him several times as Fael massaged her lower back. It left one conclusion. They cared for her deeply, and by extension, the child she carried. He couldn't fathom not caring who might be the father.

Not surprised, Strafe found no social media presence for Ian's team. He assumed they belonged to some governmental agency, and it irked him he could find no clue as to which one. He found it intriguing that neither did the woman have any social media pages.

❄ ❄ ❄

In the morning, Jesse conducted Jasirey's exam swiftly, then returned with her to his office where Fael and Liu waited for them. Jesse proceeded to the heart of the appointment—Jasirey's symptoms.

"The acid reflux and the ant-crawly sensations under my skin can become nearly unbearable," she said. "It may seem odd, but sex helps to alleviate the symptoms."

Jesse understood Jasirey's matter-of-fact answers to his questions. She needed a token measure of control in a difficult pregnancy. With symptoms uncontrollable, she could at least determine her emotional response. "Other than too little weight gain," Jesse said, "your blood pressure, glucose levels, and everything else remain on target."

Next appointment, he wanted the four husbands available to discuss the delivery. He gathered Jasirey's hands in his. "Odds are high that in another month you'll spend most if not all your time in bed to ensure those babies incubate as long as possible. Be prepared for that."

Jasirey accepted Jesse's help up off the couch as he placed his supportive hand to her lower back. She could still manage alone—given plenty of time.

Abducted

It relieved Ian when Lizzie finally agreed to visit. He credited her in part for Jasirey's acceptance of him, liked her, and wanted his wife to have every available support. Jasirey counted on Lill for friendship and scheduled lunches for girl talk with Kharia and other women from the people. They simply hadn't had time to form the seamless bond the two older friends shared.

Decked out in full makeup, Lizzie swept through the door wearing an oversize, off-the-shoulder top and plenty of glitz. It took several of the people to bring her luggage to a guest room. Everett set up tea in the living room for the women.

"Fancy house and British butler, like one of those great BBC melodramas," Lizzie said.

"Ian has relied on Everett to run his home for a great many years. He's family."

Funny, Jasirey thought. She hadn't mentioned him to Lizzie. She realized she'd given her friend few details on her marriage.

Lizzie's resistance to the nature of her marriage made it difficult to share any details. Talking about her happiness also felt like rubbing salt in her friend's still open wound concerning her husband's death. Jasirey showed her the first floor except for the pool to save that as a surprise for later.

The women joined the boys, Lee, Liu, and Fael for lunch. Lizzie hugged her godsons and goggled at the good-looking young men. She champed at the bit to give Shannon—she doubted she'd ever be able to call her Jasirey—grief about multiple sex partners. Imagine her shy, proper friend a cougar. Oh, baby.

After the meal, Jasirey sensed that Lizzie's back bothered her and escorted her to the pool. She covered Lizzie's eyes, opened the door, and prodded her forward.

"Holy shit. And a hot tub. Girl, you fell right into it, didn't you?" Jasirey raised a quizzical brow, and Lizzie rolled her eyes at her faux innocence. "A whole shit pile of gold, never mind the friggin' dinky pot at the end of the rainbow."

"Language."

"All high toned are we now, British butler and all?"

"Oh, shut up." Jasirey gestured toward the changing rooms. "You'll find a suit your size in the first one. Or what used to be your size. You've lost weight."

"Not much point in cooking for one." Lizzie wiggled her petite behind at her friend.

The loose suit bubbled up in the hot water of the Jacuzzi. Lizzie wrestled with it as Jasirey paced.

"You can actually get the big one, Lee, to plug in without being split in two?" Lizzie asked with a roguish grin.

"Body size doesn't necessarily indicate penis size."

"I hope not." Lizzie pantomimed a crude gesture, fingers splayed wide.

Jasirey batted at her friend's blond spikes. "Let's just say he has skills."

Lizzie's imagination ran a bit. "All four at once?"

"Less often now that I tire easily."

Lizzie stared. *Was she joking?*

"Hey, you're the braggart," Jasirey continued. "'Bobby had to blow air on my face to keep me from passing out from all the orgasms.'"

"Yeah, but I had one man, not four. Don't they get jealous?"

"Honestly, no. They became friends years ago and work in total sync, like taking care of me without uttering a word."

"I can't picture the juggling . . . You don't worry about the age difference?"

Jasirey's smile wavered.

Lizzie wished she'd bitten her tongue. *But be real.* She emerged from the tub and shrugged on a robe. "Nap time. Then you'll tell me about you. Where's the pregnancy glow?"

"In my stomach, fueled by acid." Jasirey led to a guestroom. "I'm glad you're here."

"Me, too. Now I'm gonna love you and leave you. I'm tired."

In her room, Jasirey turned on the intercom. She paced until the ants subsided. Then she climbed into bed. Even that task was getting harder.

Alerted by Everett, Liu checked on Jasirey, restless in her sleep. He watched a moment, debating whether it warranted waking his wife.

She bolted upright, which startled a yelp from him. He lowered beside her and decided she breathed normally, so probably not having a nightmare.

"Dreaming?" he asked.

She drew a deep breath and cuddled into his chest. "I don't remember. The dream, I mean." Weird reds, oranges, and yellows had melted, merged, and made no sense, more annoying than frightening.

Liu rubbed her back. "Do you wish to return to sleep?"

"Don't think so." She looped her arms around him. "Lizzie thinks four is decadent."

"Does she?"

"Want to play one-on-one?" she asked him.

One of Liu's favorite games.

❉ ❉ ❉

Late afternoon, Jasirey collected Lizzie and brought her and the usual snack to the garden. Silently hoping it did her friend some good, she explained her meal schedule.

"This place is huge," Lizzie said. "So, what's up?"

Jasirey knew Lizzie's disapproval lingered but that her concern for her friend pushed aside the mental chatter. Lizzie suffered chronic pain. She should understand.

Jasirey described her ant-crawling sensation that often escalated to a horrid sense of bursting out of her skin, her constant battle to eat while suffering acid reflux versus low blood sugar that challenged the potential health of the babies, and worsening pain in her lower back and groin when she stood for any length of time. Distressing her loved ones also sucked.

"Is the ant thing a panic attack?"

"No. I had those once. Woke in the middle of being intubated for anesthesia during an appendectomy. I couldn't talk, move, or breathe—terrified I'd stay awake through the surgery."

"You told me about the waking part but not the panic attacks."

Jasirey ignored the note of censure. "They didn't last longer than the recovery period. What's happening now—my body goes into overdrive for no reason, no pattern, no cause. The only emotion is, 'Oh no, here it comes again.'"

"Anything else?"

Jasirey shrugged. "The babies will be premature, which has its own risks, and preeclampsia continues to be a concern as I get bigger."

"So, barring worst case, you're sick most of the time, but it hasn't affected the babies' nor your long-term health. Does the ant and low sugar stuff happen a lot?"

"Most days to one extent or another. It'll resolve itself when the babies are born. I hold on to that. You suffer chronic pain. You manage."

Lizzie's lips puckered. "It becomes your normal. And I bitch and complain a lot." She eyed Jasirey knowingly. "You don't crow, but a big part of being able to stand this is those hunky men watching out for you." She hugged her friend. "I'm not alone either. I have you."

Jasirey's stomach moved. She placed Lizzie's hand on the ripples and smiled in dazzling joy at her friend's expression. Four rolling babies awed even the jaded.

"That should fix anyone's bad mood."

Lizzie patted her friend's belly. "Bobby died and you listened instead of mouthing useless platitudes like 'it gets better in time, think of the good memories, your family still needs you.' Without you, I might have gone stark raving mad."

Jasirey grasped Lizzie's face and turned it this way and that. "You mean you're not?"

Lizzie snorted and slapped at her friend's hands. "Brat."

When Ian returned home, Lizzie accepted — more, expected — a big hug. She had liked him and trusted him from the get-go. He didn't tiptoe. He asked straight out how she was coping.

"Good days, bad days, mostly in-between," she said.

Dinner featured a succulent prime rib, the guest's favorite. Everett served Jasirey easier-to-digest roasted chicken.

Lizzie gave Jasirey the raspberry and said, "Yuck" then "Yum" as she savored the just right rosy beef.

In perfect accord, Christopher and Michael chortled.

Lizzie saved her off-color remarks until the boys were excused. She verbally pounced at Lee. "Shannon says you're good in the sack."

His mouth dropped and his cheeks mottled.

Fael said, "Our wife fast approaches him in girth. The babies' growth squeezes her insides as well. One day, I suspect she shall snap off Lee's member altogether."

Jasirey sputtered and colored brighter than Lee, who mock swung at his grinning friend and said, "Something that won't worry you."

Fael ran a hand over Jasirey's hair. "I have received no complaints," he said.

When Everett brought in peanut butter pie, Jasirey's finger drilled into Liu's ribs. "Your idea to fatten me up?"

He grabbed her hand, swished a finger through her slice of pie and over her lips, then popped it into his mouth to suck off the residue.

"Chocolate and peanut butter," Lizzie said, cheeks hot. "Shannon's signature dessert flavors."

"I like apple date cake."

"With peanut butter frosting," everyone said.

Lizzie felt confused by erotic rushes zinging through her moldering libido as she watched the affectionate and tender touches the bantering men showered on Jasirey. At the end of the evening, she asked Ian to accompany her upstairs. "Fael, Lee, and Liu seem nice, but you can't want this. Why'd you allow it?"

Ian frowned. "It's possible you're too close to clearly see Jasirey." He kissed the puzzled lines on her forehead. "Meet some of the people from the Devoted who work here and ask for their take on her."

During Jasirey's nap the following afternoon, Lizzie visited with Kharia and Robin. "You left home for a better life here?"

"We were content at home," Robin said. "We came to serve Jasirey."

Lizzie sighed. "It's hard getting used to that name. What do you mean by serve?"

"She is destined to assure better balance in the world."

"We have a savior. We don't need another, and Shannon's the last person to consider herself some kind of prophet."

"Shannon, as you call Jasirey, is chosen by Allah," Kharia said. "Or God or Buddha, as many of the Devoted prefer. Do you not see her as special?"

"Look, I love her, but I don't understand this marriage or what you expect of her. It's a bad idea to have kids at her age. Frankly, I'm surprised she's gone along. And why hitch your wagons to her star instead of following your own?"

Robin rubbed a finger across his lips. "Americans value independence, don't they? Yet they live in a society, each individual part of the whole, though separate as the foot is separate from the hand. We Devoted, on the other hand, value duty to the whole over thinking ourselves entitled to consider only our own desires. Independence, freedom—these cannot be achieved without the help or cooperation of others."

"She is our heart," Kharia said, "but even she cannot cope without those who love and serve her, without friends."

"Friends she's got," Lizzie said. "The rest of it? Bringing balance to the world? Woo-woo stuff."

❧ ❧ ❧

Liu booked a four-night stay in a hotel for the entire family when he scheduled Jasirey's next prenatal appointment.

Jasirey planned to sacrifice her craft room for a nursery and transform the adjacent guest room into a playroom. She was grateful to be able to leave the work to Satoko and Mashita, due to arrive at the western Massachusetts compound shortly before the family's trip.

Since Lee and Fael shared computer files and paper records, they combined their offices and set up the bedroom closest to the playroom and rarely used bathroom next door for the older couple. Jasirey insisted she'd be too busy to need a craft room, but the men carted her supplies to Ian's office. With most everything he needed on his laptop, he usually worked at the table in the breakfast nook of their bedroom.

Jasirey contemplated her framed paint-by-number pictures. "I have more paintings than wall space. I should get rid of some."

Fascinated by different birds living on their land, Fael picked up a painting of a barred owl perched on a limb in a foggy wood. "If you truly do not wish to keep this, may I have it for our office? Very realistic, is it not?" he said to the others.

Lee agreed and picked a beach scene reminiscent of Samoa. Liu chose a sun-bathed birdhouse guarded by the parents of a baby bluebird. Ian liked mated wolves sunning on a ledge.

Jasirey blushed. "You guys are kooky." Her imp surfaced. "And you, my Ian, what office will you put yours in now?"

He lifted an eyebrow. "I do have another office."

"You're kidding. You can't put a paint-by-number in your business office."

"Title on the door says otherwise."

Jasirey grabbed at the painting. Ian grabbed her and planted a kiss on soft lips.

"Mine," he said.

Jasirey knew he didn't mean the painting.

Satoko, looking more vibrant than the last time Jasirey saw her, and Mashita exclaimed over Jasirey's baby belly, the lovely house, and the magnificent grounds. The next morning, they began perusing baby paraphernalia catalogs and agreed on a cheerfully whimsical motif for the nursery. They asked artists among the people to design a Noah's Ark mural, a learning tool for animal names, colors, and numbers. Mashita and Satoko supervised ordering and placement of the selected furniture.

Several security people accompanied the family to Boston in two vans, one driven by Robin. They had booked a large suite that included several bedrooms, since the men planned individual sleeping dates with their wife. They spent the afternoon at the New England Aquarium, where Jasirey most enjoyed brightly hued coral-reef fish and delicate seahorses.

For dinner, the family ordered room service, a fun novelty for the boys and, a surprise to the men, for Jasirey.

"We rarely went on vacations," she said, reclining as ordered on the couch in the sitting room. "Maybe the occasional weekend at inexpensive motels with no room service."

At bedtime, the men gathered about Jasirey. Lee hugged her good night. Her belly bumped into him, and marveling at how far it bulged past his hands, he knelt to cradle it. "I was not squashing you," he said to the children to be. "It's rude to interrupt."

Jasirey kissed him. "I love you, teddy bear."

Kissing her stomach, Lee received a kick. "Disreputable children." His cheeks dimpled.

Fael framed her face for a loving kiss, and Liu nuzzled, rubbing a hand over her belly.

Alone with her in his room, Ian lifted Jasirey. It thrilled her that he could. "How did you get first in line?" she asked him.

"I cheated." He waggled his eyebrows and set Jasirey laughing on the bed. Sinking to his knees, he circled her hips and more inclined to cuddle than indulge in sex, rested his head on the little of her lap left.

Knowing he enjoyed it, she gently scratched his scalp.

He helped her undress and spooned with her on the bed, caressing her ass that he considered lovely, though it seemed to shrink in contrast to her growing belly.

Jasirey dredged up the courage to broach a subject long on her mind, "Ian?"

He murmured drowsily.

"Have you actually spanked anyone—the sensual, sexual kind, I mean?"

The unexpected question woke him up. "Why do you ask?"

She rolled a bit laboriously to face him and rested her head on his arm. A soft blush further intrigued him.

"You always threaten, and when you guys visited the island, I fantasized about you spanking me. I wondered if the reality had any similarity to the fantasy." Her blush deepened.

Adorable woman and, despite four lustful husbands, still so innocent, he thought. "I don't want to hurt you, baby."

"Oh, well, don't want to be hurt. Just curious."

"This fantasy, did you get off to it?"

She ducked into his shoulder, but he'd seen the spark of excitement in her eyes.

"Tell me," he said, his voice husky.

With the arousing story, Ian no longer felt any lack of energy. He looped an arm under her belly, dragged her to the edge of the mattress, and drew her upright. One palm circled the peaks of her breasts as the other caressed her from neck to ass. "Don't go anywhere," he whispered, nipping her ear.

Jasirey quivered in anticipation. As her comfort and wellbeing had become even more of a priority to the husbands, Ian fetched cushions from a small sofa and along with pillows laid them on the bed to create a supportive nest for her belly. She left one foot on the floor, placed the other knee up on the bed, and rested her forearms on the cushions to support herself.

Ian fondled her ass cheeks. "I think it unwise to try spanking in your condition. I have a gentler idea in mind. Tell me if you don't like it." He smiled as her hands began kneading the sheets.

Ian covered her ass in butterfly kisses, then carefully raked his teeth over satiny skin. He breathed in her warm response, bore down against his aching hardness, and concentrated on not bruising her. He bit gently on a mouthful of flesh, sucked a few seconds, then continued in another spot until Jasirey's cheeks turned a delicate pink.

Ian entered her warm wetness from behind and swirled his hips, his hands skimming Jasirey's tingling backside. He drove her crazy. She urgently pushed back into him. He set a gentle rhythm, one palm tapping her ass, the other holding her hip. Before long, both gasped for breath.

Ian knew a powerful orgasm brewed in Jasirey and clasped her hips to help hold up her weight. His own body bucked fiercely through Jasirey's strong spasms. Buried in her tight heat, he carefully dragged her body off the cushions and onto her left side. A few more gyrations, and he slowly withdrew. She fisted around him once more.

Very nice, they each thought in concert.

❧ ❧ ❧

Jasirey had a midmorning appointment. Robin and the security people stayed on the boys' heels as they followed the red brick markers of the Freedom Trail beginning at Boston Common, the oldest city park in the country.

Jesse greeted the men and Jasirey in his private office where he asked them to sit on a couple of sofas.

"How have you been?" he asked Jasirey.

"You already know. I bet my husbands tell you every detail."

"True," he said. "Now tell me what they don't know."

"Smart aleck." She smiled. "The weight's harder to hold up. The baby bulge makes sitting uncomfortable, so I lie around. I read a lot of books, but I feel like an incubator." At her husbands' aggravated expressions, her imp added, "Sex is still pretty amazing."

Jesse's eyes crinkled. "Glad to hear it. No spotting, cramps, or contractions afterward?"

Jasirey shook her head, and Lee, Fael, and Ian exchanged glances.

Why hadn't they been warned to watch for such symptoms? They would corner Jasirey for a husband-wife chat later, they thought as if one mind.

Jesse felt the byplay but remained on track. "As long as that remains the case and no preeclampsia symptoms arise, I won't tell you to restrict your sex life."

Fael dropped the psychological blocks he usually used to prevent being overwhelmed by others' feelings and was inundated by the deep concern Jesse masked.

"Gentlemen," Jesse said, "risks in a pregnancy of multiples include premature birth and preeclampsia or full-blown eclampsia with possible long-term damage to the mother including convulsions or coma."

Coma and convulsions? Long-term damage? Dear God. The men forgot any annoyance in their sole desire to protect and care for their wife.

Jesse addressed Jasirey. "I assume you're a sensible woman who understands taking it easy equates to maintaining her health and that of her babies."

"Subtle you're not."

Jesse winked at the men and informed them, "Birth plan—multiples rarely reach maturity in the overly stretched womb or even during the adequate but not optimal thirty-seven weeks for the systems of each newborn to work independently.

"They will require specialized neonatal care." he told them. "Ian says you have a house here. You should move into it this coming month. We'll schedule an appointment for a caesarean and be on the lookout for labor symptoms. We want to avoid vaginal delivery. We can discuss today's ultrasound at dinner."

The families had planned to go out that evening. Jesse managed a moment alone with the men while an assistant handled Jasirey's vitals and scheduled tests.

"Gentlemen," Jesse said, "Jasirey has reached a critical stage. She'll be on complete bed rest soon. Find ways to occupy that busy brain and prevent emotional stress that will translate to extra physical stress her body can't tolerate."

Confident he'd done his job and scared the shit out of them, he patted their shoulders. He expected no further friction or undercurrents for the duration of the pregnancy.

He hadn't exaggerated his concerns.

❧ ❧ ❧

The family met Jesse and Lill at a parking garage near the restaurant with an entrance on a side street containing several small businesses, the others closed at that time of night. The street ended at the garage, and the restaurant's back door opened to a narrow alley that turned back onto the street.

As part of their security protocol, Fael and Lee had checked out the location before making reservations. In the middle-class neighborhood, little crime had been reported by any of the businesses. The street was wide enough to mount a defense if necessary, and the two-tier parking garage had better than average lighting.

At the casual family eatery that served rolls, sticky buns, and corn fritters with warm syrup before diners' meals arrived, Jasirey indulged in a bun and hoped the rest of the dinner would offset the sugary treat.

The men dominated the conversation, discussing football, a game Liu and Fael found barbaric. Lee appreciated the skill involved. After dinner, the debate grew as the group returned to the garage. Lill drew Jasirey to a storefront displaying costume jewelry. Shadows on the glass warned of danger too late.

Harsh hands suddenly clamped over Jasirey's mouth. Dragged through the store and out the back to the alley, she nearly retched at the putrid stench from a dumpster. Pushed against a scratchy wall, she used the discomfort to distract from her roiling stomach.

"One sound and your friend dies." Jasirey's abductor shifted to allow a glimpse of Lill, eyes wide in terror, a knife held to her throat by an accomplice.

The kidnaper released his captive's mouth. "Jasirey." Disdain rolled through the syllables. "You're smaller than I envisioned."

Jasirey noted the British accent. "You've made a mistake. My name's Shannon."

87

"Lovely name." Jet eyes glittered. "Your men construct quite the security system for your home. Won't do you much good, I'm afraid." He nodded at the man holding Lill.

Shoving a cloth to her face, Lill's tormentor let her collapse unaided to the filthy street.

Jasirey's captor set a hand on her belly and laughed at the flaring fire in her eyes.

"Don't worry, Mama Tigress. You carry precious cargo." He grabbed her arm in a bruising grip. "Valuable cargo."

And that was entirely the wrong thing to say.

Doubting the man could support her weight and praying for her babies' safety, Jasirey went limp. She fell heavily, knocked the man off balance, and lifted her legs to drive them piston-like into his stomach. His grunt of exhaled air pleased Jasirey as he flew into men rushing to his aid.

Jasirey let loose a scream that pierced even her own ears.

The man snarled and, fists clenched, bulled forward. Jasirey flung her arms over her belly.

Cursing her, the man yanked her arm to raise her up. She remained limp. Others joined him to brutally haul her to her feet. The slap of pounding feet following them through the store galvanized them into action.

❧ ❧ ❧

Raging at how long it had taken the men to realize the women weren't behind them on the empty street and to find the one open door where they could have been taken, Lee roared his frustration at a cargo van speeding out the far end of the narrow alley.

While listening to his cell phone, Fael held it chin to shoulder and signaled Lee. "Kimika has Jasirey's tracking signal quickly moving away from us. She is in that van."

Lee gave a terse nod.

Jesse ran to Lill and examined her with shaking hands.

Liu sniffed. "Chloroform. We can care for her at the hotel."

Ian squatted beside Jesse. "Trust us to handle this. Jasirey's life depends on it."

Jesse saw determination banking fury in Ian's dark eyes. Jesse grabbed his arm. "If the birth comes unattended, none of them will survive."

Robin turned their van into the alley. In the back seat, Christopher and Michael clutched the seats in front of them. Ian carefully lifted Lill so Jesse could climb into the back to hold her. The boys' tears ripped a wider hole in the men's hearts. Ian sat next to the teenagers, and Liu took the driver's seat.

"We'll get your mom back," Lee said. "Can you hold on till you get to the hotel? Lill needs attention."

Though sniffling, the teenagers settled. Lee closed the van door and handed Jesse's car keys to Robin, who sprinted toward the parking garage. Lee gave Liu a two-fingered salute and watched a moment as the van began its return to the hotel where Ian and Liu would care for Lill and the boys and inform the Imperiat of Jasirey's abduction.

Fael and Lee had two security people scour the alley while they searched the store. They expected the cargo van had a stolen license plate, a dead end.

Other than the point of access, a broken window in the back, nothing else in the store answered their questions. Whoever had kidnapped Jasirey had the technical knowledge to bypass the store's alarm, but why they had taken Jasirey or how they knew the family would be at the restaurant were questions that would have to wait until they found her.

That they would was not in question.

❧ ❧ ❧

Eric sat in the cargo hold of his van with three of his men and one eerily mute captive scrunched into a corner. He had expected screams, expletives, and threats followed by pleading. The woman, however, remained silent. And watchful.

Eric allowed himself a few moments to gloat. Happening by chance to have seen an article in a gossip rag about Ian's marriage, he immediately put out digital feelers to locate the happy couple—not an easy task, since none of the men nor the woman were on social media. He had found clues on the sites of some of Ian's employees and set things in motion to worm his way into Marcus's good graces with the intention of moving up in the trafficker's organization.

He then searched for exactly the right hideout—a log cabin for hunters deep in a Maine forest where drones could not operate and only satellite phones worked. And, of course, no neighbors.

Setting up surveillance of the woman's comings and goings had been the tricky part. She seldom left their western Massachusetts compound. Nor did the people who worked there. A vital avenue of information therefore closed to him. When he followed them to the hotel and the family's evening plans became clear, final details for abducting her fell into place.

Eric noticed that the longer they drove, the more pale his captive became. He saw her wince several times as the van hit potholes on the little-used back roads they chose to get to Interstate Highway 495. He offered no comfort.

❧ ❧ ❧

Sitting on the bare metal floor in a corner of a cargo van, legs pulled up beside her, Jasirey shivered, her back and legs screaming in protest. She distracted herself by studying the kidnappers sitting in the back with her. The leader, thirtyish—not Marcus, the man who had accosted her in the dress shop—perhaps worked for the trafficker, which was a wild guess, but she knew of no one else who had threatened her.

The leader's black, shaggy hair waved around finely drawn features and coldly pleased eyes. Three others, ranging from mid-twenties to thirties, had nondescript features and coloring. None looked pleasant.

It was hours before the van thumped onto an unpaved track meant for utility vehicles. Refusing to cry out, Jasirey dug her elbows into the walls to brace herself. The rough ride continued bump after bump. The van finally stopped, and one man grabbed under her arms, another at her ankles. She gritted her teeth as they carried her into a cabin surrounded by dense forest, through a sitting area/kitchen space, and into a narrow, windowless room where they dumped her onto a cot.

Just past the bed sat a stained toilet and sink. Redolent of bleach and the mildew embedded in the rough log walls, the room made Jasirey's throat tickle. She mustn't cough. She desperately needed the toilet but feared her legs might crumble. The leader stood over her. Jasirey refused to ask him for help.

Eric assessed his pale captive. Beads of perspiration dotted her upper lip and forehead. He considered sending a picture to her husbands.

"My name is Eric," he said to her. "Do you need anything? Perhaps some aspirin? Marcus will want you nice and healthy." He laughed at her

90

quickly indrawn breath. "Know about him and his vendetta against your men, do you?"

Gauging his hard, obsidian eyes, Jasirey chose the safer course of saying little and shook her head. After the click of a lock outside the bedroom door, she rolled on creaky springs and inched her legs toward the floor. She took even, deep breaths as she waited for the room to stop spinning, then shifted her weight to wobbly legs. Vicious spikes in her groin and lower back raised silent tears. Leaning heavily on the splintering log wall, she shuffled forward the few steps to the toilet.

At home, the husbands had installed toilets with handicapped features for her. The toilet in her cell-like room looked like a toddler's potty chair. As she straddled it, Jasirey's leg barely fit between the bowl and the wall.

She washed her hands and drank water that tasted of iron from the faucet.

Jasirey reclined on her left side and pressed her back into the cool wall for relief. Her pain eased, allowing her to think. Yes, she knew about the human trafficker Marcus's grudge against her husbands because they more than once stopped him from kidnapping children. She had also met him at that dress shop and would not soon forget the cold calculation in his grass-green eyes—probably disguising contacts—as he assessed her pregnancy.

In the hands of people solely interested in revenge and perhaps profit from selling her babies, neither she nor they were likely to survive. She could accept whatever fate awaited her but not the fate Marcus intended for her children. Jasirey shivered under the one thin blanket and prayed through the endless mid-September night for guidance on the few choices she could see.

One thing she knew for sure. She would not allow Marcus to have her babies.

At Fael's request, the Imperiat immediately sent Kimika and the detail of men and women he now commanded to Maine and an area of deep forest where the husbands had lost the signal of the tracking device Liu had slid beneath Jasirey's skin near the armpit the night of the Imperiatu. They had a search area—acres worth with no mapped roads.

Arriving at the edge of the forest, Kimika, coordinating with Fael and Lee, had his squad enter on foot at daybreak. They searched for Jasirey's signal as well as the track the kidnapers' van must have used so the husbands could follow with a similar van filled with a small bed and medical supplies to transport Jasirey out.

Kimika separated his squad to search several sectors at a time, following Jasirey's signal when found and patiently, doggedly backtracking or changing direction when it lessened or disappeared. Around noon, six hours into the search, they found a promising track to follow and soon picked up Jasirey's signal. The husbands followed with the van.

Choices Are What Make Life Difficult

Come morning, Eric made Jasirey's decision for her. She heard the snick of the lock and bolstered herself against the wall. He carried in a tray.

Not bothering to mask a smirk, he said, "Why, you don't look rested, Mrs. . . . there are so many possibilities. Whose name do you bear?"

She ignored the gibes. "What do you plan for the babies, Eric?"

Babies—plural. That, the calm in those blue-green eyes, and his name on her lips unsettled him, a reaction he didn't appreciate. He summoned a nasty smile but felt it dim under the woman's indomitable stare. His jaw jutted forward. "When you're ripe, we'll cut them out and sell them to the highest bidder."

"I see." She said nothing more.

Eric slammed out the door before he did her physical violence. *Damn the whore.*

Jasirey flushed the food down the toilet and slept until another man brought in lunch and removed the breakfast tray without a word. She shakily disposed of lunch as she had breakfast.

❧ ❧ ❧

By midafternoon, Eric had mastered himself and entered the woman's room. She had her back to the door. With the swollen belly not as evident, she looked a good deal smaller.

Determined to keep his wits about him, he said, "It's a pleasant afternoon. Would you care to walk outside?"

He heard a faint, "No."

He forced her onto her back. "What's wrong?" he asked. He felt her cold, deathly pale, damp skin and hair. Eyes closing, she again faced the wall. He grabbed her chin and jerked her head toward him. "You tell me what's wrong."

93

"Don't know," she said on a wispy breath.

"Fuck," he shouted. "Damn whore! Marcus won't thank me for a corpse."

Disconnected thoughts tumbled through his mind: she knew what he looked like, he should get rid of her in the woods, leave her, no one would find her in time.

The kidnapper's panic broke through Jasirey's lethargy. The faint hope died that when he recognized she was ill, he would take her to a hospital. Trying to concentrate felt like walking through deep water. Finally, she forced a bridge from her mind to his. "Leave me," she whispered and gathered her little remaining strength to push the thought deep into his consciousness. He walked out the door, and she felt a knife-like twinge deep in her belly that pitched her into darkness.

❧ ❧ ❧

Tethered to monitors and dimly feeling hands soothing her, Jasirey struggled to wake. Liu's name wavered on her long wail.

"Shush, darling. You are safe. Everything is fine."

"No, I felt something happen."

"You are spotting, not uncommon. Our children's hearts beat as strongly as their mother's. Jesse wishes you to stay in the hospital one day for observation only."

The restrained passion in Ian's kiss shouted the full extent of his terror.

Lee's kiss held gratitude. "We informed everyone you're okay. The boys held on."

Liu's smile faltered. "Precious one, why did he not feed you?"

Jasirey closed her eyes. "His name is Eric. He said he would sell the babies. I couldn't let that happen."

"I do not understand."

Fael guessed what she had done, and knowing his anger was fueled by terror, fought to keep it from spilling over. "We have extensive resources of which you are unaware. We would never stop searching for you."

Liu caught on and carefully stopped clutching at Jasirey's hand. "You are not alone. You must do everything you can to survive and trust us to find you." Tears spilling down his wife's face prevented Liu from saying anything else.

Later that evening after conferring with one another and remembering Jesse's warning against stressing her, the husbands decided not to further press Jasirey about allowing her sugar level to drop to the point where she could have died.

They also decided not to inform her of the tracking device, for although excelling at keeping feelings and thoughts to herself, she was a lousy liar when confronted.

❧ ❧ ❧

After being released from the hospital the next morning and arriving home in western Massachusetts, Jasirey saw a sea of people waiting for her in the driveway. She trained on her sons. If possible, she'd have run to them. They ran to her and grabbed hold. She kissed them repeatedly until their tears mingled.

Arms trembling, Everett embraced her. "I worried for you." She pressed her cheek to his.

Kharia and Robin kissed Jasirey's cheeks as did their pink-faced sons. Satoko, Mashita, and a host of the people—her extended family—welcomed Jasirey home but soon dispersed to let her rest. Unable to face being cooped up in a room, even one as large as their bedroom, she asked to go to the pool. Not advised to swim, she floated on an inflatable alongside her husbands and sons, who remained close.

Before dinner, Liu whisked Jasirey to the bedroom for another checkup. He placed a stethoscope on her belly. "Sounds good."

Running fingers through his hair soothed her as petting a cat would. "Tell me you understand my decision."

"My precious one, promise to have faith and wait for us, and we shall move on."

Jasirey closed off the hurt. Her husbands disapproved of her having courted low blood sugar to thwart Eric's plans. *Get over it,* she counseled herself.

At prayers, Michael and Christopher were unusually vocal in their thanks for getting their mom back safely. After the boys went upstairs, Kimika and his security team joined the family in the living room. Kimika knelt, bowed, and kissed her hand.

"Kimika now heads our home security personnel," Fael said.

Then Kamika assisted her to stand and introduced his people. *Very young,* she judged. Since their unexpectedly abrupt posting to America, they maintained an unrelenting at-attention posture.

Jasirey attempted to put them at ease. "Thank you for coming. Consider this your home now."

The group saluted and bowed. Jasirey placed a restraining hand on Kimika's arm as they left. She reached up to hug him. "I didn't want to embarrass you in front of the others, commander," she whispered.

❧ ❧ ❧

At seven months, Jasirey's belly hampered her every movement. She didn't remember being that clumsy when carrying Christopher or Michael even at nine months. Supporting the weight of quadruplets downright hurt. She rested comfortably only in the pool.

The husbands often watched her play, singing and poking at the bunching and bulging under the stretched skin that increased with her touch, which at first disturbed Ian, Lee, and Fael. Jasirey laughed at their worries. Never had she been more beautiful.

Lill and Jesse visited the next weekend. Relieved to see no injuries from their ordeal with Eric, the women clutched at each other. Jesse gently pried them apart to examine Jasirey. He ordered no exercise other than walking in the pool. He affirmed that she could float on an inflatable.

Not wanting to get smacked, Jasirey's husbands wisely left unsaid that they found her pregnant-belly waddle adorable. As they told Jesse, the pain was a different story.

"She uses the pool to ease her joint pain," Liu said. The water helps alleviate the feeling of ants crawling on her skin and inside her, and the discomfort subsides to a manageable level."

"Manageable," Lee scoffed. "I detest that word. Not many could tolerate our wife's definition of the word."

When being examined by Jesse, Jasirey tried to make a joke of her reservoir of guilt that deepened each time she failed to prevent herself from snapping at her husbands.

"Good thing there's four of them," she said. "My crankiness gets spread out to smaller doses."

Jesse leaned in conspiratorially. "Just tell yourself, 'I'm in this position because of them.'"

The following day, Lill and Jasirey had lunch in the craft room near a window overlooking a small garden. Brilliant reds, oranges, and golds of a sugar maple flecked the fading green. Streaming last season's Super Bowl in the living room, the men renewed their interrupted football argument.

Halfway through the meal, eyes on her plate, Lill asked, "Did that man hurt you?"

Jasirey squeezed Lill's hand. "No. He, Eric, planned the abduction to give me to a human trafficker who resents my husbands for interfering in his business. Eric hoped to advance in the trafficker's organization."

A hand to her throat, Lill said, "I couldn't have stood it if they'd hurt you."

"Me, neither—you, I mean. Can I tell you something in confidence?"

"Of course, honey."

"I haven't mentioned it to my husbands. I'm not sure why."

Lill stopped eating.

Jasirey pulled a card from her pocket. "It's from the trafficker, a man named Marcus." She handed it to Lill.

She read, "Be assured madam, that I did not authorize Eric to accost you nor will the foolish man do so again. I will allow no one else to orchestrate our next meeting. Marcus"

Jasirey also told Lill about the nudge she had given Eric to leave her behind.

"I'm not surprised," Lill said. "That weekend we stayed with you when your husbands were away, I became very upset at not being able to do much for you. Peace, warmth, comfort flowed into me and certainly wasn't from inside me. It came from you."

Lill reached for Jasirey's hand. "It scares me this bad guy Marcus could be obsessed with you. He sounds more dangerous than the kidnapper."

Jasirey agreed but said nothing about her strong hunch that Eric would not do anything again in this lifetime.

❧ ❧ ❧

Jasirey regretted that her restlessness woke her men and suggested one sleep in the bedroom, the rest in their offices. The men flatly refused. She gathered the remnants of her tattered humor and teased that they had to be rested to plug the babies in to nurse at night as she slept. They thought it might be prudent to practice the plugging-in technique.

For Jasirey, the one comforting constant in a debilitating pregnancy had been her emotional need and physical desire for her men. As she got bigger, they all simply cuddled. Less physicality allowed their concerns for her health and the babies' welfare to bleed through as well as their disappointment involving the whole Eric fiasco—their word. She didn't know how to counter that.

She understood their difficulty in accepting that she put her own and the babies' lives in danger by allowing her blood sugar level to plummet instead of waiting for them to find her, and maybe she did react too quickly, but they hadn't been there to help her make what in the moment felt like a damned pressing decision.

Jasirey realized that her restlessness at night woke her men and contributed to everyone's deteriorating mood. She again suggested one sleep in the bedroom while the others could sleep better in their offices.

The men gave a token argument, but then finally acquiesced to her request and found the arrangement restful and a refuge from daily pressures.

Jasirey rarely let her health interfere with her sons' after-school visits with her. The second time they asked to be excused from a visit to their father, she said, "What's up, guys?"

"It's not that we don't like it at his house," Christopher said.

Michael rolled his eyes. "He's got a girlfriend. She says it should be family time—no friends. We can't even play video games."

Jasirey hid a smile. *God forbid, no video games.* "You've talked to your dad?"

Christopher's peaceable tone hardened. "He does whatever she says."

"He's whipped," Michael said. His mother swallowed a laugh. "He asked us to stay for a week at Christmas."

A week. Since the attack by Eric and despite Jasirey's confidence that he no longer threatened her, she had to force herself not to clutch at them when hugging them goodbye for their visits with Roger. Still, she managed a light tone. "The babies will be here then. You may wish yourselves far away from crying newborns."

"I'll stay in my room," Michael said.

Christopher elbowed him.

"What, you want to change diapers?"

A burst of laughter lessened Jasirey's anxiety. "I won't force you to spend your vacation at your dad's, but I expect you to tell him how you feel. As for your brothers and sisters, infants don't make good playmates, and I think we'll spare you diaper duty."

"Sweet." Michael pumped his fist, and Christopher grinned.

"You can talk to them, help them recognize you as big brothers." Jasirey assumed her best mother's glare to say, "No teaching them to swear."

"Come on, Mom," Michael said. "That's the fun part."

Christopher tried to look innocent.

Poor babies are going to be corrupted, Jasirey thought.

Destiny Sucks

Jasirey's mood turned along with the coloring leaves. She battled irritability, tears, and remorse for her temper. The men were at a loss. Sympathy aggravated her. Their advice about her health made her snap at them and, in the next breath, apologize. They learned to shut their mouths, finally figured out she needed a distraction, and called Lizzie.

She arrived loudly. *Dumb men, what do they know about pregnancy moods?* Lizzie watched for a few seconds as Jasirey paced in the pool. "Hey, bitch. How come those four men of yours can't handle one lone pregnant woman?" Her friend's brittle laugh had Lizzie plunging in to hug her.

"Holy shit." Lizzie's arms barely reached past the belly. "How do you haul that around?"

"Ever see a beached elephant seal?"

Lizzie stretched to kiss Jasirey's cheek. "Poor kid."

Jasirey rested her forehead against Lizzie's. "It's gotten so hard."

"Shan, it's not much longer."

Jasirey's return smile more closely resembled a grimace.

"Sex still amazing?"

Jasirey pointed at her belly. "All this weight pressing down on my groin, lay a finger on me, and I'm off."

"Great, rub it in the face of the old broad not getting any."

The constricting lump in Jasirey's throat ebbed. She placed an arm around Lizzie's diminutive shoulders and led her from the pool. Jasirey's robe reached round her boulder belly and dragged on the floor in back. She waved Lizzie toward the whirlpool.

"Yes, baby. I dream of hot tubs. Maybe I'll move to someplace that has one. Fresh start. Everything drags me back to Bobby being sick—his chair, his side of the bed. Last week I found a bag of his medicines in the chair pocket. I've got to move forward, find something to do."

"You'd be wonderful at consulting."

Lizzie, a paralegal prior to her disability, had the honor of having one of the legal briefs she drafted result in a finding that became a precedent for others to use in their cases. She missed the challenge of pitting her research and deductive skills against that of the opposing counsel.

During Jasirey's morning nap the following day, Satoko, eager to please the one friend from their lady's past who had visited, showed Lizzie the nursery. Oak bureaus, changing tables, and cribs provided a dark contrast to azure walls and white puffy curtains.

Lizzie palmed a crib rail, real wood. "Shannon used to buy tacky pressed-board stuff and didn't mind the difference. Bet Ian picked these."

"Our lady, my husband, and I chose the furnishings."

"You've got good taste. Why do you call her lady? She's not English high society."

"She is important to us."

"Look, I know Shannon. She's no . . . this pregnancy . . . it was her choice, wasn't it?"

Satoko's glittering eyes softened. "She suffers greatly. Friends to distract are a blessing."

"I hope so."

Lizzie stayed several days and endured some of Jasirey's moods, which she thought her friend admirably restrained. She said to the men, "Suck it up. She's nearing the end of her tolerance. Let her spew, rant, and rave. You guys can take it."

Lizzie kissed their cheeks and demanded a call first thing after the newborns arrived.

❈ ❈ ❈

Jesse and Lill visited the compound for the weekend. Since Jasirey showed no signs of preeclampsia, Jesse believed his patient blessed despite the evident deterioration of her ability to emotionally handle the stresses on her body.

She retired early, loudly insisting that her husbands stay to entertain their guests. The men stared at her retreating back.

Jesse glanced at Lill. Both burst out laughing.

"My God," Lill said through tears of laughter, "she's spoiled you men."

Ian's eyes narrowed.

Jesse raised both hands for peace. "Babe," he said to Lill, "give them a break. They're first-timers. Was I any wiser our first pregnancy?"

"Not that I recall and not much better the second time."

"Hey." Jesse accepted her kiss of apology amidst her subsiding giggles. He gave the men a rueful smile. "Our first child made me a better doctor. I understood the physical states of pregnancy. Lill initiated me into the mental side—fuzzy-headedness, mood swings, irritability. Sorry honey. Even occasional irrational outbursts. Your wife's especially strong protective instinct may have mitigated such side effects till now."

Lill eyed the four men. "Jesse was a nervous wreck during my pregnancy, had a few emotional meltdowns of his own. I haven't seen either in you fellows."

"Thank you, honey," Jesse said. "I missed that. With a caesarean, birthing classes are unnecessary. I assume Liu is teaching you childcare."

"We studied child development on the island," Lee said confidently.

Jesse pinned a stern look on them. "Not the same thing. Months of debilitating illness, then surgery, and you expect your wife and one couple to care for four newborns?"

"We expect to help," Ian said evenly.

"Really. Explain how to change a baby with an umbilical stump."

Ian had no idea what it was let alone the procedure for handling it.

Jesse pointed at Liu. "Get dolls and show them the proper way to change, bathe, feed, and hold premature newborns." He looked at the husbands. "Learn parenting skills, strategies for colic and such."

Facing the others, Liu apologized. "I focused on supporting Jasirey through the pregnancy and pushed aside the hands-on care of the infants. We are woefully unprepared."

"Maybe we coped by ignoring the inevitable," Lee said.

"It's nicer than meltdowns," Lill said charitably.

They discussed the move to the Boston house where Kimika had set up a security system.

Informed by her husbands that Jesse suggested it was time to go to the city, Jasirey said, "I'll go in three weeks."

"The babies may decide to appear at any point," Jesse said. "It isn't safe to wait."

Lee wrapped her in his big arms. "We're moving in two days, little one."

Jasirey's head banged against his chest. "I'll go crazy without the pool."

Jesse patted her shoulder. "I doubt the babies will permit time for that."

The Boston house had no elevator, so they transformed the downstairs den into a bedroom for Jasirey. A bathroom with a portable handicapped toilet seat sat across the hall. Her feet no longer visible to herself, Jasirey required assistance in and out of the tub to shower.

Jasirey didn't mind the cramped conditions. She'd mostly lived in smaller houses, though they contained fewer people. The boys' teacher, Everett, and Kimika's squad had accompanied the family. Kirani and Bazir joined school lessons from the compound via Zoom. Without the buoying water of the pool, Jasirey spent her days reclining on the couch in the living room, a stack of books and a basket of crochet supplies beside her.

Liu bought preemie-sized dolls for the soon-to-be fathers to begin cramming baby know-how into resistant brains.

The third time he ripped through a palm-sized diaper, Lee cursed under his breath—he'd learned some anatomically explicit ones in America—and argued that nothing human could fit into such miniscule packaging.

Ian's confidence withered as Liu warned him several times that he could break the baby's neck if he didn't support it properly.

The men learned the facts of changing diapers including cleaning boys versus girls and care of umbilical stumps. They all, including Lee eventually, thought the little notched diapers were brilliant. Breast feeding versus bottle feeding—they'd have to feed with bottles since Jasirey could not constantly produce milk for four.

Sudden infant death syndrome—Fael, Lee, and Ian all panicked at that one. Babies sleeping on their backs and no soft items in the cribs to press against their small faces hardly seemed an adequate remedy to the three men. They considered taking turns keeping watch at night. Liu suggested a baby monitor.

Last, the five Ss for fussy babies—swaddling, placing them on their sides, shaking gently, shushing to imitate the sound in the womb, sucking. And none of that included emotional and intellectual nurturing. Their heads spun.

Jasirey sat or, rather, lay in on a couple of the trainings.

Her luminous eyes while recounting stories of the boys as babies sent impatience rearing in the men to see their babies in her arms.

❧ ❧ ❧

To distract herself, Jasirey invited Charlotte to visit. They talked about families, and Jasirey asked, "Have you ever been married?"

"I tried a marriage that conformed to my parent's expectations," Charlotte said, "a husband satisfied with a clean house, dinner on the table, and an amicable divorce. He had plenty of alternates in the wings. I explored relationships with women but then met Ian. He needed my skills and recommended me to the Devoted. They became the unconditionally loving family I craved. Now, I enjoy being single, connected to family and friends who don't live with me."

Jasirey laughed. "Studies of heterosexual couples show married men live longer than unmarried and vice versa for women. Wonder how that works for same sex couples."

❧ ❧ ❧

Evenings, Fael often worked on his wife's legs, the tremors running beneath the skin tangible to his fingertips. Though not lessening the crawly sensation, massage provided something else to concentrate on. She said it helped.

To be sure, Fael dropped the blocking techniques he used to keep others' emotions from overwhelming him, especially his wife's with her stronger ability to perceive what others felt. As a result, Fael received a disquieting jolt. He could read nothing from her and later apprised Master Kai of the development.

The older man tapped his lip. "This escalation in mental control no doubt stems from her treatment when kidnapped. The lore on Jasirey offers little insight into guiding our current lady." He assessed Fael. "Have you called to request assistance with her training?"

"I suspect she has progressed beyond my expertise."

104

"You believe she has developed the tools necessary to control gifts she has not yet perceived in herself?"

A testament to Fael's control, he did not squirm under Master Kai's impassive gaze. He buried his foolish doubts in a bow. Jasirey needed him, someone who thoroughly understood her, someone she implicitly trusted to guide her into the present phase of her destiny.

❧ ❧ ❧

That evening, Ian sat on the floor, his back against the couch. Fael massaged Jasirey's legs. While scrolling through financial reports on his laptop, Ian described the companies belonging to his corporation.

Jasirey became quiet, and Ian assumed she'd fallen asleep. He jumped when a slender finger pointed. She asked if those items normally ran to such similar amounts.

"Excuse me?" Amused and then stunned, he read as Jasirey tapped the keys to scroll back to pages where she had seen the anomalies. She pointed out a series of columns on each page. Eyes narrowed, he jumped up to grab his phone.

Slightly sorry for the head or heads about to roll, Jasirey sighed. *Dumb-dumbs.*

"Perhaps it was a mistake of some sort," Fael said.

"Too concise and methodical. I worked in office management until the boys arrived."

Fael contemplated his wife. "I have difficulty imagining you at a desk day after day."

"I'm efficient and organized, good for administrative assistance." She made a face. "Little room for creativity, but you work to afford the things you prefer to do—hobbies, travel—or simply to pay the bills."

Fael's eyes sharpened at Jasirey's shy smile that portended a confidence.

"I had intended," she said, "before the Devoted and becoming pregnant, to pursue one of my dreams. Guess it'll stay on the shelf a while longer."

"What dream?"

Fael thought she would brush the question aside, but instead, she said, "I write journals about the boys that I'll give to them on their eighteenth birthdays. And one for myself—thoughts, insights—I might one day turn into a book."

Ian knelt beside her. She searched his eyes. "You okay?"

"Thanks to my observant, brilliant wife."

"Do you know who worked on the pages with the discrepancies? Anyone you were fond of?"

"Leave it to you to worry about my heart instead of dollar amounts and business consequences. What clued you in to the problem?"

Jasirey repeated what she'd told Fael.

"An oblique pattern," Ian said. "My accountants missed it. I'd never have caught it if you hadn't shown me."

"Seemed pretty clear to me."

Ian shared a smile with Fael. "I've given the matter to an associate I trust so I can concentrate on family."

Jasirey gripped their hands. "It's good to be king."

Fael snorted.

"Boost, please. I'm tired, I need a snack, and I've got to pee."

Well versed in the priorities, the men lifted and pointed her toward the bathroom.

❁ ❁ ❁

Roger planned a party for Christopher, Michael, and their friends for Halloween. Christopher's grisly zombie costume sent a shudder through Jasirey. Michael picked a video-game character with fake swords too realistic for her taste. Thankful they'd grown past trick-or-treating, Jasirey nonetheless struggled to eat and sleep when they went to their father's and, despite knowing security shadowed her sons wherever they went, every time they left the Boston house.

Fael decided it was the perfect opening for suggesting she begin training. Building on her breathing techniques, he taught her how to focus on her body's reactions—pulse, muscle tightness, breath changes during heightened emotions and how to use her breathing to stay in control of her body and thereby her ability to assess any problem and determine a remedy.

Jasirey took the training seriously. She might not like manipulating people as she had the kidnapper to make him leave her unharmed in the cabin, but she would do it to protect herself or her children.

❁ ❁ ❁

November arrived on a bitter cold front that refused to budge. No less stubborn, Jasirey delayed the caesarean until Jesse refused to put it off again and scheduled it in two days' time. With snow forecasted overnight, Jasirey hoped for another delay, but bad weather would be no match for Ian's gas-guzzling all-terrain vehicles.

By morning, even Jasirey had to admit that more than two feet of snow qualified as overkill. She loved the fairytale look of trees bowed with heavy white snow topped with sparkling ice. Unfortunately, overloaded branches snapped, blocked roads, and pulled down power lines. The city and suburbs came to a standstill, and the Governor declared a state of emergency.

Electricity and phones had gone out overnight, so the household used the fireplaces and set up battery-powered lanterns.

With school canceled for the day, Jasirey encouraged her husbands to take Christopher and Michael outside for sledding. The property boasted a small hill safely bare of trees. Most of the people, many unfamiliar with winter activities, joined them. The teens took gleeful advantage.

Snow in Massachusetts tended to be light and dry and not good for packing. That day's wet snow made excellent snowballs for splatting down collars and into mittens. To the boys' disgruntlement, the people soon got the hang of returning the teens' fire.

Once snow on the hill compacted, sleds flew wicked fast. Intermittent flakes of snow continued falling, but not feeling terribly cold and fortified with Everett's homemade cocoa, the group stayed outdoors for hours and created an army of inventive snow people including bikini-clad snowwomen and Poseidon with his trident.

Taking the longest time by far, everyone gathered to build a fishing boat of snow replete with a ladder—steps scooped from the side—a deck people could walk on, and a pilothouse big enough for two people to enter.

As the other husbands played outside, Liu paced inside the house. Jasirey bade him sit on the floor beside the sofa and ran calming fingers through his hair. His head bumped her distended abdomen. Pressing his cheek to it in apology, he jerked upright and placed both hands on her belly. "Are you in pain?"

"No, my Liu, I'm fine. Relax."

His eyes bored into hers. "Describe the pain."

Annoyance crept over Jasirey's small face. Liu rubbed her back. "Is it the same as yesterday or when you woke?"

"You mean my back? It gets worse as the day goes on. You know that."

He had left a hand on her belly. "Precious one, do you not feel the contraction?"

"Probably those Braxton-Hicks ones." Her eyelids drooped.

"Perhaps." He kissed her forehead. "Sleep, darling."

Liu drew Kimika to the kitchen where Everett prepared hearty sandwiches and asked him to fetch the other husbands. The red-cheeked men tramped in, stomping snow from their boots. Liu sent Kimika to watch over Jasirey.

"She is in labor," he said without preamble.

Kimika shouted for Liu.

Jasirey cried softly and struggled to get up. She had vomited.

Mindful of the small, alarmingly clear puddle, Liu knelt beside her. "Rest a minute."

Lee and Ian walked Jasirey to the bathroom and then the bedroom. At his request, Everett fetched her Liu's nutrient-dense smoothie.

"Haven't been sick in a while," Jasirey mumbled. "My back hurts."

Lee rubbed small circles over it. He lifted worried eyes to Liu since he knew back pain often indicates labor.

Liu fingered a lock of hair from her eyes. "Sleep. Lee shall stay with you."

Outside the door, Ian said, "I thought she shouldn't have food if in labor."

"She ate little of her breakfast. The small amount of vomit contained only water. A drop in glucose level has the potential to intensify labor. Our goal is to slow things down until we can transport her to the hospital." He called Jesse.

"Nothing's moving out there," the doctor said, "and news reports state that emergency services are stretched to their limit. Help Jasirey stay calm and pray labor doesn't escalate before conditions improve. Getting stuck on the road is not something we want to chance."

Liu gave Jasirey another smoothie at lunch, which pleased her, since her appetite had vanished. She asked to return to the living room. Lee carried her as she gripped his neck to whisper, "Don't worry, my teddy bear."

He beckoned the others to gather about their wife.

"Definite contractions," she said, "but erratic and far apart. I take it getting to the hospital isn't an option."

"Work crews are working on the problem, loved one."

"Poor husbands, you look scared to death. We can do this."

"We have no way to ascertain the position of the babies." Liu's voice came out more clipped than intended. He caressed Jasirey's hair. "Precious one, they will require specialized care, to which we have no access."

She smiled. Unnaturally calm, the men thought.

"Let's prepare as best we can," she said, "and trust things will work out as they should. Kimika, ask the boys' teacher to keep them busy this afternoon and, from the top right-hand drawer of the bureau in my bedroom, get me the Protectors' statue, please. Liu, can you perform a caesarean?"

His mouth opened and closed. The burning fervor in Jasirey's eyes failed to thaw the icy tentacles gripping the men from heart to testicles.

Kimika returned shortly and reached to set the small fertility symbol on the mantle. He nearly dropped it when Jasirey said, "Listen, if we're forced to do this here and things go wrong, promise you'll put the babies' welfare first."

Liu's eyes wheeled until Jasirey laced her fingers through his. Calmness and confidence flowed through him. Mindful of his vow as Jasirey's Protector, he answered carefully. "We lack the necessary equipment and medication for a caesarean. If the birth is imminent and you cannot survive, I shall do everything possible to ensure the babies' survival."

"Fine distinction, but I promise to accept your decisions and never blame you. You promise not to blame yourself for whatever you may be forced to do, okay?"

Eyes closed, Liu nodded.

"Ian?"

He dropped beside her.

"Be their commander and take some of the burden of decision from Liu. Save the babies."

Under her gaze, nothing seemed impossible. "I'll stay at your side and his."

"Tricky answers, but I'll take them. I love you, my wonderful husbands."

Lee and Fael's dread of what she alluded to eased at her quiet courage.

❧ ❧ ❧

At midafternoon, still without power, Jasirey easily breathed through the contractions beginning to strike at closer intervals. Her back killed. The men switched between ice cups kept in snowbanks and massage. Jasirey stayed on the couch, which Everett protected with a plastic tarp and a sheet.

Suburban road conditions hadn't improved. A rebound snow squall added several more inches, and frigid, incoming night air further hampered work crews.

When Jasirey's water broke, the contractions built. Refusing to leave his lady's side, Kimika placed lanterns against the gloom.

Liu examined Jasirey and found her cervix dilated several centimeters.

Having stayed prone to slow the process, Jasirey said, "Liu, help isn't coming. Should I walk and speed things along? At some point, I'll lose the energy to focus."

Liu called Jesse who agreed with Jasirey. Time for these babies to be born.

Everett hung towels and sheets on laundry racks next to the fire to warm them for the arriving newborns. The men sterilized sharp kitchen shears and set out supplies they might need from Liu's medical kit.

Since an upright position facilitated delivery, Lee and Fael cobbled together a semi-reclining birthing chair with belts attached to footrests to keep her feet and thereby her legs steady and a seat that supported the buttocks and thighs but left the front open for Liu to catch a newborn. They placed other necessary items—gloves, stethoscope, sterilized string—on the scrubbed coffee table.

Jasirey noted the absence of a knife but said nothing. If it came to that, sterilization wouldn't matter.

Ian and Lee lifted Jasirey to her feet but stood still as an immediate contraction forced the air from her lungs with a soft grunt that would become familiar. Short term, walking relieved her straining muscles. Her legs soon wobbled, though, forcing her to lie down.

Her breathing changed depending on the strength of a contraction. Using the fire as her focal point, she maintained an impressive focus, the men thought. When Jasirey worked through contractions, Fael wiped her face, a simple gesture that gave her immense relief. Constant breathing dried her mouth, and Fael fed her sips of warm liquids kept by the fireplace or applied balm to her chapped lips.

Jasirey weakened faster each time she got up. Hours passed and the cervix dilated to ten centimeters. She leaned on Lee and Ian to walk to the birthing chair and straightened abruptly.

"I think there's a head in the canal," she said.

In the chair, Liu examined her—definitely a head.

"All right, darling, push on the next contraction."

Jasirey gripped Lee and Ian's forearms, breathed deeply, and bore down. The contraction subsided, and she rested. Another contraction, a few more, and the head crowned. Liu inserted gloved fingers into the vaginal opening and, to prevent tearing, carefully stretched it past the small head.

Ian, Lee, and Fael held their breath as Jasirey prepared to push again. Head and shoulders through, Liu supported the baby's neck. In the next contraction, the baby left its mother's body. Liu rubbed the tiny back and turned the newborn face-up.

Voice hoarse, Liu said, "Firstborn is a boy." He suctioned the child's nostrils and handed him to his mother.

"Hello, baby," she cooed.

"Can we touch him?" Lee whispered.

Jasirey quickly handed the infant to a startled Lee and painlessly passed the placenta. Liu caught it in a bucket, tied and cut the cord, and then returned the newborn to Jasirey.

Love glowed from her to the little boy and his father. "Ian, meet your son, Colin Everett." Ian's father had been named Colin.

Tears pooling, Everett kissed Jasirey's cheek and took the baby to weigh him. Ian hovered at his heels. Everett stood on the scales holding the infant and subtracted his weight, a crude estimate he added to the child's name, sex, and time of birth. He supervised Ian's first time diapering and swaddling a live infant.

A well-formed child, Colin blinked alertly at the men. After a few moments of cuddling, Ian laid him in a basket near the fireplace.

Instructed to stand guard and ensure that the baby's breathing remained normal, Kimika stared starry-eyed at the precious bundle.

Jasirey breathed through several lesser contractions. Liu examined her ever so gently. "No head yet. Rest on the couch."

As Jasirey lacked the strength to walk, Lee carried his wife. "Colin is beautiful, little one, and you are beyond courageous."

"My Lee, I'd gladly let you guys take over."

He nuzzled her cheek. "We haven't your power to endure." Her grip on his hand tightened. Differences in contractions evident, he said, "A strong one." He thanked God Jasirey remembered breathing techniques from her previous labors.

"How long between births?" she asked Liu.

"Natural births of multiples are rare. Your body will guide us."

After another strong contraction, she slept a bit. Afterward, she walked with Ian and Lee's support. An immediate hard contraction and another zapped her energy. Liu checked the babies' heartbeats whenever she rested. Before long, another head protruded through the cervix, and everyone moved to the chair.

"Bear down, precious one." The baby arrived in less than twenty minutes. "A girl."

Jasirey cradled her red-faced, squalling baby. "This is Jaimie Lee." Jasirey's love shone at Lee from a face translucent with fatigue.

His finger fit nearly ear to ear over his little girl's damp head.

Everett weighed and cleaned the child as he crooned to her.

Liu examined the baby and found her healthy and strong.

Lee cradled her until she slept in his arms. He reluctantly placed her next to Colin.

Jasirey fell asleep on the couch. Both newborns were larger than expected and breathing well. Liu had the men pray for their wife and the babies still to be born.

Two hours later, Jasirey realized things had gone wrong.

Daddy Dilemma

Pain steadily worsened and the urge to push harder to fight. Jasirey blessed Fael's attentiveness as perspiration dewed her face.

Liu examined her and tore his gloves off to lay his head in his hands. The others tensed. Jasirey lost focus in a strong contraction and pushed. Liu grasped her hand.

"Liu, I can't . . . too long. What's happening?"

"The baby is not in proper position. The cord protrudes through the cervix."

Her words came in gulps. "So, push it . . . you can do . . . turn it."

"To attempt this mid labor, the pain—"

"Get . . . lot worse." Jasirey's breath rasped on a long contraction. "Please, Liu."

"What must be done?" asked Fael.

Liu grabbed Fael's sleeve and led the men out of earshot of their wife. "It means manipulating the baby from outside of Jasirey's abdomen while continuously monitoring whether the cord has wound around the child's neck. We have no ultrasound equipment to show what is happening inside the womb." Liu's voice cracked. "I am delivering blind and cannot do both tasks together."

"Guide me, I have the smallest hand," Fael said. "I can examine Jasirey as the child is delivered."

Liu's ruddy cheeks cooled. "Yes. Good. Yes, that leaves me free to manipulate from the outside and align the baby. You can use your fingers to check around the neck as the child emerges."

Fael scrubbed. Liu pushed an extra long glove up to his elbow.

Lee gathered Fael for a hasty, one-armed hug. "Courage, little man."

Ian laid Jasirey on their portable massage table, and Lee gently dragged her hips to the edge. Blood thundered in their ears as they each supported one of her trembling legs. Fael fought to center himself. None of the men had the courage to face the suffering in their wife's eyes.

"My loves." Comforting warmth—motherly love, Jasirey's absolute love for them—cascaded through the men.

His empathic senses deluged in her pain, exhaustion, and fierce determination, not even Fael registered the power Jasirey projected to calm them.

"All will be well, beloved," he said. He let everyone's emotions wash through him and then concentrated solely on the child's safety.

"Gentlemen," Liu said calmly, "let us deliver this baby."

Time suspended as they focused on Liu's instructions to Fael while he massaged Jasirey's deflating belly to maneuver the child through the birth canal.

If able, Jasirey breathed. She moaned when unable. Everett wiped away her sweat and tears or pressed down on her shoulders when they strained against hideous pain. He prayed, pleaded, that her body be able to withstand this brutal assault.

Kimika's eyes remained on the babies, his ears attuned to every breath, every sound from Jasirey. *How can she endure this?*

Fael felt the head bulging through the cervix. The men lowered the top half of the table for Liu to stand behind Jasirey and support her in a sitting position. He pressed down on their wife's abdomen with each contraction until Fael could ease a finger around the child's neck.

"The cord is not around the neck," he said, "but it sits on the child's shoulder."

Liu took a moment to think. "All right. Gently move the cord away as the baby comes down, then immediately remove your finger and prepare to catch the child."

Two minutes later, an olive-skinned girl slid into Fael's hands. He laid her on her mother's lap.

"Fael," Jasirey said in a wispy voice, "you delivered your daughter, Safia Souzan."

Tears flooding his face, he gazed adoringly at the tiny newborn. Souzan had been his mother's name.

"Take her."

"Do not push," Liu warned. "Breathe."

Too late. The placenta passed. A head crowned right behind it, and the last, a boy, rushed into the world. Jasirey named him Sun Li after his grandparents, Li Sizhu and Sun Xiyang.

Everett let loose a whoop of relief every man there silently echoed.

Ian whispered. "It's over, baby. Four healthy children. You did it, brave, remarkable girl."

Liu ordered Ian to raise the table in place. Hurtling the men back to reality, he said, "The bleeding is heavy with swelling and small tears, though I do not believe she requires stitches. Bring the babies to nurse to stimulate uterine contractions and slow the bleeding."

Liu carefully cleaned Jasirey. "Lee, carry her to the bedroom."

"Can't I stay here?" She wanted the fire and the Protectors' fertility statue on the mantle. They had kept her focused and able to cope.

Lee, Ian, and Kimika dismantled a full-size bed in ten minutes and reassembled it facing the fireplace. Kimika carefully propped their lady on pillows. Jasirey's eyes flared, her back arched, and her teeth gritted against a silent scream.

❋ ❋ ❋

Jasirey never spoke the name of the stillborn child. She'd heard of the birth defect—anencephaly—missing the top of the head, only the brain stem formed. The tiny body looked mummified, as though dead for some time. Jesse said no, but Jasirey knew something had happened during the kidnapping. She decided to cremate the body and spread the ashes in the garden come spring. She named her baby girl Iana.

Mashed and mangled, Jasirey lay, barely able to move. The newborns woke as pale sunlight parted the clouds in pearly paths down to the earth. Jasirey's eyes appeared to have suffered several punches.

The husbands gallantly schooled their expressions to hide their pity. She wanted to use the bathroom but couldn't lug her legs past the bed's edge or sit upright. The men found her tearful aversion to the bedpan unfathomable.

"Baby," Ian said, "you actually believe you ought to be able to control this after the trauma your body has endured?"

"If I've been through a trauma, why do I have to be rational?"

The men melted, and Ian cradled his anything but fragile wife in his arms. "No reason I can possibly think of." He rocked her while planting kisses on her wet face.

When the babies needed changing, the men found wriggling infants a far greater challenge than dolls. Dressing them in onesies and the caps, booties, and sweaters their mother had crocheted for them, each husband cared for a baby other than the one designated as his to ensure equal bonding. They never doubted Jasirey's knowledge of the children's parentage.

Lee cradled Colin in one arm, unbuttoned the top of Jasirey's nightshirt, and assisted in holding the baby to her breast. Colin made breathy snuffling noises and latched on after a few attempts. He appeared so much bigger next to his mother. She winced.

"Does it hurt?" Lee fretted, unable to bear her having to endure further pain.

"Just the uterus contracting." She gave her son five minutes and kissed his downy cheek.

Colin squawked a bit. "Never mind, little man," Lee said. "I have what you need."

Everett had sterilized glass baby bottles. Jasirey first nursed a child for five minutes, then released him or her to one of the fathers who offered a bottle of formula to the baby. Jasirey looked teary each time she had to hand over an infant.

Lee said in singsong, "I know what you're thinking. Colin, your mama bear hates not being able to fully feed you." She whapped the large arm not cradling Colin. Lee barely felt it.

Ian held Jaimie to Jasirey's other breast. The infant latched on instantly and sucked with enthusiasm.

"She knows what she wants," Ian said, "just like her mama." He laid his cheek lightly on Jasirey's head. Torrents of emotion—the horror of watching his beloved in pain, the thought he never let fully form that they might lose her in childbirth— coursed through him to her.

Jasirey snuggled a moment longer. "We're all right, my Ian."

He kissed her lightly and sat on a chair to give Jaimie her bottle. Jaimie gulped at it.

Liu assisted Safia. Floundering, she fussed, and he guided her.

Fael held Sun Li, whose baby noises made him sound delighted by the offering before him. Jasirey and Fael laughed, a welcome and cleansing sound to everyone.

Sun Li latched on, lost it, gazed blearily, and lunged.

Jasirey squeaked in protest. The baby settled, and she leaned her cheek against Fael's. "You guys are kind of scruffy," she said as she patted his bristly face and nestled against his shoulder.

Fael smiled. "The babies gave us no time for personal grooming this morning."

Jasirey became serious. "You saved me, Safia, and Sun Li. Thank you, my Fael."

"No, loved one, your incomparable courage saved us all, for we cannot do without you."

❧ ❧ ❧

They brought the babies to their mother in reverse order throughout the day to ensure that each newborn received an equal share of immunity-building colostrum. As before, Jaimie latched on easily. The rest struggled, the fathers fondly plugging them in. As she'd predicted, Jasirey was incapable of keeping her eyes open, though her pregnancy symptoms dissipated at a speed that amazed Liu.

Everett mixed water and rubbing alcohol in plastic bags and froze them in the snow, forming a thick sludge.

The cold packs provided lifesavers to Jasirey's challenged body. Better rested twenty-four hours after the births, she scrutinized each child.

Colin inherited Ian's large eyes and had big hands and feet, a thick thatch of dark hair, and pale skin. He weighed the most yet looked tiny.

Jasirey ran tender fingers across his head and smiled at Ian. "Did you have beautiful hair like your son's?"

"Well, it was dark, and I did have some."

Jaimie had a moderate amount of dark brown hair and a rosebud mouth. Jasirey hoped Safia's hair turned her father's mink-soft sable and her eyes to Fael's golden hue. With his happy baby noises, Sun Li enchanted her much as did Liu, his mischievous father. Her own playfulness rose.

"It required weeks for the boys to latch on to my undersized nipples. These babies lucked out that their fathers were resolved to stretch them."

She laughed as her men groped for a reply.

❧ ❧ ❧

Michael and Christopher came to meet their siblings. They tentatively hugged their mom who they worried looked pretty bad, as

117

did her weirdly deflated belly. Michael worked at not biting his nails and clasped his hands tightly when told about the stillborn baby. Christopher crossed his arms.

"It's all right," their mother said. "We're blessed to have these little ones, and I'm grateful for each one of them."

Demanding to be fed, Jaimie screamed. Jasirey draped a baby blanket over herself for her sons' comfort, though not her privacy. Circumstances of the births had placed a moratorium on her obsessive modesty. Unable to ignore the gross sucking sounds, the teens turned pink.

Lee presented Safia. Michael and Christopher silently acknowledged that she was cute, and Sun Li made them laugh. They thought Colin resembled Ian, sort of. All in all, the babies weren't too bad, though the boys had a hard time thinking of the squirming arms and legs as brothers and sisters.

❦ ❦ ❦

Power was restored, and the main roads were cleared a few days after the storm.

Jesse arrived and hugged the men in congratulation to give himself time to adjust to Jasirey's appearance.

He gently kissed Jasirey's chalk-white cheek, and she knew their doctor-patient relationship had firmly rooted into a friendship akin to family.

"I'll get back to you," Jesse said, "after I examine the babies." He carried a scale and equipment to sample blood into the kitchen and set up to examine the infants.

Their hearts and lungs worked perfectly, he concluded, their bodies well formed with normal muscle and eye reactions. Each child weighed more than five pounds. He couldn't imagine how Jasirey's small body had held them. Mother and children seemed a miracle. He pronounced the infants healthy and adorable.

Jesse examined Jasirey and recommended plenty of rest, a nursing mother's diet, and frequent short walks. Exhaustion and weakness after such a birth and difficult pregnancy would linger for some time, he knew. Nursing further depleted Jasirey's energy, but Jesse accepted that she'd ignore any suggestion to totally bottle feed the newborns.

"Other than obvious soreness and expected weariness," he said, "you're fit as a fiddle."

"Other than. I can hardly lift my arms, let alone get up and walk."

He smiled kindly at her. "You have no shortage of helpers."

"No more bedpan?" She gloated triumphantly at her men.

"To the bathroom and back will count as a walk," Jesse said in amusement. He handed her presents from him and Lill, the first a heavy set of four baby books to chronicle the babies' milestones.

Four. A nanosecond of blankness, then Jasirey said, "Nice. Thank you, Jesse."

The second gift held undergarment onesies. "Lill says you can't have too many of these, though if memory serves, we found unopened packages when we cleared out baby things."

Jasirey loved the last offering containing chewable books and toys for the babies.

"Thank you, Jesse, and please thank Lill for us," Jasirey said.

Jesse realized Jasirey's energy had tanked. He handed Ian legal papers to sign and promised them birth certificates before they returned to western Massachusetts. Drawing Liu aside, Jesse advised, "Watch for signs of depression and other repercussions. Chronic fatigue alone will wear on a person, especially one used to being active."

❈ ❈ ❈

The Devoted in the Boston house joyously adopted the American Thanksgiving holiday. Everett and Jasirey had decided on several smaller turkeys that provided more wings and legs. Everett had brought vegetables from the farm. In the Devoted tradition, thankful prayers waited for the end of the dinner.

Several choked on their passionate emotions. They left it to Jasirey's husbands to voice everyone's gratitude for healthy newborns and to request safe passage for the lost one.

Afterward, her stomach blessedly acid free, Jasirey rested on the couch. Lee joined the boys to play racing video games he enjoyed no matter the vehicle type, and Ian worked on his laptop while Fael and Liu lazed on cushions in front of the fire.

Jasirey observed her men relaxing. The last months had exacted a toll on them as well. "You guys are awfully pretty in the firelight. You look especially handsome in those reading glasses, my Ian."

The answering gleam in the men's eyes spiked a fight-or-flight response Jasirey clamped down before consciously registering it.

Ian closed his laptop.

She gingerly scooted down to give him room. With sitting upright still a short-term undertaking, she lay with her head on his lap.

Sun Li voiced waking noises from his bassinet by the fireplace. He rarely cried. Fael changed him, then laid him in his mother's arms.

Jasirey sang rhyming nonsense to him. "Sweet boy, Mama's pride and joy." She laughed at his responding burbles. He seemed to want to sing along.

Lee came downstairs as the rest of the babies woke. The fathers sat on the floor by the couch to feed the infants. They had been right. Seeing their babies in Jasirey's arms warmed their hearts.

Eyes lighting, she smiled at them.

"Trouble," Fael said.

Her innocent, "What?" fooled no one.

She targeted Ian. "Are you Daddy One, Two, Three, or Four?" Yup, not a clue. "You can't all be Daddy. Kind of confusing."

"What will they call us?" asked Lee in dismay.

"Chinese children call their fathers Baba," Liu said. "I shall speak Mandarin to ours in the hope they become multilingual."

"The Arabic word is the same for daddy. I shall use the more formal Ab," Fael said. "I suggest, however, that we seek guidelines for introducing languages to the children."

"Good idea," Lee said, "though in my case, Samoan isn't a language used much outside of Samoa. What about Dad for me and Daddy for Ian?"

Jasirey's head wagged. "Kids don't say daddy past a certain age."

"I never cared for Father," Ian said.

Lee agreed. "Too formal."

"Pop?" Jasirey repressed a giggle.

Ian's lips twitched. "If you can't be helpful, be quiet."

Lee's eyes twinkled. "I'm your teddy bear. They may as well call me Papa Bear."

"Good. I'll be Dad," Ian said, "and hopefully, Daddy for a good long time."

Jesse decided to go to Jasirey for the next checkup and bring Lill along before she hounded him to death. Jasirey slept, so he examined the babies.

Lill managed to peck the men's cheeks before descending on the newborns. Jesse wasn't blind to the longing in her eyes. He drafted his wife as an assistant. The infants had gained weight, had normal test reactions, and soon fussed to be fed.

Lill embraced a waking Jasirey. "Hello, darling. They're gorgeous. How are you?"

"Fine. Four healthy, wonderful babies. I'm blessed."

Babbling to them nonstop, Lill fed Colin and Safia. When Jasirey finished her part of the feeding, Jesse led her into the bedroom for her exam.

"You're healing well," Jesse said. "Sitting becoming easier?"

"I get tired, a little sore, but I can lie down in the limo if necessary. I want to go home. Christmas is almost here."

"The babies should tolerate the plane trip home."

Jasirey's eyes widened. "I completely forgot about the plane."

"Forgot you're no longer pregnant?" She paled, and he said, "Jasirey, what's wrong? And don't tell me, nothing."

"I can't do this again."

"I don't follow."

"Another pregnancy."

"Of course not. Why does that concern you?"

"They expect me to have five live ones next time.

Jesse sputtered in shock.

Jasirey sighed. "To be fair, it was my vision. I saw these four and five the second pregnancy."

"That's ridiculous and extremely dangerous."

"They consider it a done deal. Will you tell them their hopes and beliefs are ridiculous?"

"Oh, you bet. Anyone suggesting you go through this again should be horsewhipped." Seeing her woe-be-gone face, Jesse calmed himself. "Listen, they love you and want you safe. We'll schedule an appointment for after Christmas and discuss birth control options."

"I'm sorry to lay this on you. Come for New Year's. I promise to be better."

"Nonsense. I'm your doctor. Anything that affects your health, I want to be informed. I'm also a friend in awe of your perseverance and courage. I understand why the Devoted chose you." He wiped her glistening eyes. "Your hormones have shifted. That and coping with the stillbirth, I expect you've had lots of these. We'll stay on alert, make sure the blues phase doesn't last too long."

When Jesse rejoined the husbands and Lill, the men bombarded him with questions.

"Her hormones level at this stage," he said, "playing havoc on the emotions. She's healing well, though she'll require more than the average six weeks for recovery. I think she and the babies can fly home." He turned to Lill. "She's invited us for New Year's Eve, honey, if we have no other plans."

Lill smiled in fond exasperation. She'd told him of their plans but doubted anyone could pass up the chance to see those babies again. She got up to help serve the cake Everett brought in.

"I'll examine Jasirey again when we're there," Jesse continued. "In the meantime, no sex."

Lill pretended an absorbed interest in the plate on her lap—not embarrassed—to grant the men the illusion of privacy.

Ian shuddered at the persistent vision of his wife's body struggling to give birth.

"Dear God," Lee mumbled.

Determined to afford Jasirey every possible comfort, Fael said, "And the pool?"

"When the bleeding subsides. Walking is best for now."

❧ ❧ ❧

After an easy plane trip, correctly installing four car seats in the limo at the airport required more effort but eventually succeeded with each baby safely in place.

When they arrived home, Satoko and Mashita—enamored at first sight—ensconced the babies in the nursery. Kharia ushered Jasirey into the pine-scented living room where a tall blue spruce spread across the French doors.

Ian fitted himself to his wife's back. "I had a smaller tree set up in our room."

"Thank you, my Ian." Jasirey loved decorating for Christmas, though as she was still recovering, she might only hang ornaments. She turned to snuggle.

"It still feels strange not having a belly poking into me."

"I'd rather have the babies."

"No question." Jasirey rested safely in his arms, Ian's best Christmas present.

❄ ❄ ❄

The next day, between baby feedings and changes with Satoko and Mashita shortening the process considerably, the men retrieved boxes of Christmas decorations from the attic. Jasirey hung her handmade decorations—crocheted lacy snowflakes, delicate see-through covers over jewel-toned balls, and a popcorn-cranberry garland—on the bedroom tree. Christopher and Michael hung ornaments they'd made or had a sentimental attachment to on the tree in the living room.

Jasirey asked Lee if he wanted to place a menorah on the fireplace mantle. "I'd like to include traditions from everyone's beliefs," she said.

"I agree," Lee said, "but not this year. When the babies can participate will be the time to introduce family traditions. Christopher and Michael's are already established."

On the family's third day at the compound, the people welcomed the newborns. A proud Satoko and Mashita helped carry the infants downstairs.

The people considered the introduction a solemn occasion and quietly presented a mound of gifts. But tiny hands and feet waved, milk bubbles popped, and alert little eyes captivated the adults. A competition soon waged to draw the babies' attention.

Her warm skin tone a nice reminder that pale was not her normal complexion, Jasirey looked lovely in the firelight. The people presented a wreath of holly and baby's breath to her for the missing child.

Rooted to her seat, Jasirey struggled to breathe until her babies fussed to be fed. Holding their warm little bodies eased the stricture in her throat. The people drifted off as she nursed the infants, and Satoko, Mashita, Kharia, and Robin returned the infants to the nursery for bottles.

Ian sat next to Jasirey and handed her a red box tied in gold ribbon. "Very pretty," she said, "but daddies don't have to give presents."

"And all the lovely things you made?"

The baby afghans with a panda bear, lions and lambs, ducklings in sailor suits, and dinosaurs outlined in colorful popcorn stitches especially impressed her husbands.

Jasirey opened the small package. Delicate gold charms of each child's name, including Christopher's and Michael's, shimmered in the lights.

"Fael will attach them to the chains of your bracelet" Ian said. "They're meant to resemble a webbing of lace. Baby, do you want one for—"

"This is perfect. Thank you, Ian."

Fael handed her a larger package. "From me, Liu, and Lee." Nestled inside sat four balls of gleaming, sculpted copper strips caging miniature, carved wooden cradles. One of the babies' names and the year labeled each cradle in ornate script.

"Their first Christmas ornaments. They're beautiful."

Lee handed her the last package, a set of five hardcover journals. "Fael told us of the books you write for Michael and Christopher. We bought these before the birth and meant the fifth one for your personal thoughts. Is it all right?"

Jasirey hugged each of her men. "Thank you."

As the men gathered up the party litter, Jasirey gently laid Iana's wreath on the fire.

❧ ❧ ❧

Sick of being sick or at least not well, Jasirey chafed at the endless healing process. She had little pain or discomfort, just no energy. Easy physical tasks wiped her out. Unsure what her condition would be after the birth, Jasirey had finished her handmade gifts beforehand. Christopher and Michael had grown past making decorations or Christmas cookies, so feeding and playing with the babies provided the highlight of her days. Satoko, Mashita, and her husbands handled the physical chores.

Fearing overburdening the older couple, Jasirey drew the line at them assisting during the night. They dug in, she commanded. Tears pooling in their lady's eyes were more coercive, and the couple complied gracefully.

Ian planned to stay home through the New Year but spent several hours on the computer each day. Neither did Lee, Liu, or Fael's duties end at fatherly chores. The men retired after family prayers and the bedtime feeding. They'd be awakened soon enough for the next. Jasirey wondered if exhaustion equaled a deliberate defense against abstinence. She missed their usual cuddling.

The effort to keep up a conversation wearing, she called Lizzie less often. Lizzie barely remembered her first Christmas without Bobby and could drum up no enthusiasm for the present year. Nevertheless, her son and daughter insisted she join in on the family celebrations.

Relieved, Jasirey stopped worrying about her friend. She spent the time unclaimed by the children in her craft room watching the bird feeder placed outside the window for chickadees, cardinals, and blue jays. Waiting for spring, she placed Iana's ashes on a shelf and wrote a paragraph in the children's journals about the sister none of them would meet. Extensive pages in the babies' journals described their daily growth and loving daddies and brothers. She included a poem that years earlier she'd written for the boys.

The Beginning of Being Begun

Complements tumble.

Meet in oneness,

Grasp tenaciously.

Moored suspended,

Bulge and flutter.

Grow snug,

Push outward,

Perfectly completed.

❊ ❊ ❊

The books the men had read explaining the feeding schedules of newborns had not prepared them. Even during missions before they met Jasirey, they'd mostly maintained regular sleep patterns, so the relentless interruptions to their sleep as new parents took a toll on them.

Ian caught himself nodding off at his laptop and resorted to power naps to stay focused. Jasirey appeared rested, despite tiring easily, and remained even-tempered while caring for hungry or cranky babies. He didn't miss the pervasive anxiety of the pregnancy nor Jasirey's irritability and adored listening to her sing to them.

Ian imagined no better family life.

Lee rarely napped but fell asleep within minutes of his head hitting the pillow. He reveled in fatherhood from dirty diapers to marking distinctly evolving traits in each child. Lee enjoyed listening to Jasirey read palm-sized books to the babies—in reality, her commentaries on the colorful pictures—and reading to the infants as well.

Fael suffered most from the lack of sleep. His metabolism required an hour or two of extra nightly rest. He napped when feasible.

The babies' alertness increased daily. Jasirey said the lifting of the edges of their lips did not yet constitute smiles. Fael did not quite believe that. Pleased her discomfort had abated, he no longer required emotional blocking in her closed-off presence. He attributed her occasional vacant expression to weariness from recovery. For the time being, he suspended the energy-intensive mental training practices they had begun.

As a healer, Liu had often been summoned in the night. It did not prepare him for the every-few-hours call to wake up. The people learned, unless an emergency, not to disturb him midafternoons in the infirmary.

Liu found the babies advanced for their age and extremely good looking. He adjusted to Jasirey no longer requiring his constant care. Her body healed well. She ate healthily, though she cared little about what was placed before her and faced the chaos of parenting with tender efficiency. Her calm demeanor assisted them in coping.

The dads found themselves most taken aback by the powerful emotional tug the newborns engendered, the fierce protectiveness. They had experienced similar feelings, particularly during Jasirey's capture, for Christopher and Michael. The instinct intensified for helpless, dependent infants.

Return to the Island

Christmas morning dawned gray and gloomy. The fire and twinkling tree looked all the more inviting. Per family tradition, the boys opened their five-foot long stockings when they woke while gifts under the tree waited until the adults got up and everyone had breakfast.

Christopher and Michael itched with excitement. Used to inexpensive bulky presents—socks, underwear—to fill up the huge stockings—unexpected gifts including a guitar tuner and a popular band's CD in the stockings heightened anticipation for what there might be under the tree.

The fathers laid the babies on a thick blanket to watch the multicolored lights. The room smelled of pine, cinnamon-scented candles, and a buffet breakfast set on the coffee table.

Satoko and Mashita, wearing the warm coats and boots the family gave them, left to spend the day at the people's dormitory. Everett took part in the family celebration.

The teens hugged their mother and stepdads in thanks for the stockings and, despite being full of junk food, devoured waffles covered in greenhouse strawberries and whipped cream.

Stockings Jasirey had filled for the men boyishly excited and embarrassed them since one for her had never occurred to them. The teens unhelpfully mentioned that their father hadn't done it, either.

Since the babies lacked for nothing and understood none of the fanfare, the husbands skipped gifts for them. They deferred to Jasirey's holiday traditions. Ian played Santa, one present handed out at a time, opened, and appreciated by everyone.

The boys bought their mother a teapot painted in lilacs; their stepfathers, mugs decorated with their animal spirits; and Everett, a mug with a collage of the teens' favorite foods. They took pride in getting a laugh out of the dignified older man.

The men gave the boys traditional martial arts practice clothes and a racing game Fael overheard Lee and the teens discussing, his friend likely to have as much fun as the boys. Having raised two sons, Everett knew what teenagers liked and found the highest capacity water guns available, canons to Jasirey's mind. The family bought him an open-ended ticket to London.

Conspiring with her husbands, Jasirey made good her desire to spoil the boys for Christmas. Christopher was overcome by a twelve-string guitar and Michael by an iPod.

Jasirey had crocheted a lap afghan for Everett which made a cozy accessory for the e-reader from the family. She gave her husbands handmade sweaters and vests.

Not used to New England's prolonged cold, Fael, Liu, and Lee especially appreciated them. She also bought each a gold ring embossed with his animal spirit. The men kissed her until the boys complained that it was supposed to be family time.

Ian gave Jasirey an ivory gown, a spray of lilacs decorating one side of the bodice and the opposite hip. From China, Liu had ordered an iridescent silk shawl hand-embroidered in daffodils. Fael sculpted a metal wall hanging of the garden in full bloom including the fountain and a swing that swung.

Everett had found a bottle of perfume, its stopper an iris. Jasirey applied a dab and her husbands sniffed, stirring a pot Jasirey wished left alone. She shooed them back.

Lee stepped out and returned carrying a large box topped by an even larger bow. He placed it in front of Christopher and Michael. "From all of us."

The boys grabbed at it.

"Easy."

Christopher removed the lid carefully and stared, hardly believing his eyes. The teens had given up begging for a puppy. Their mother, unable to afford the vet bills, had resisted buying pets.

Not wanting to frighten the quivering ball of fluff, the teens spoke softly and petted his fuzzy head. The Saint Bernard jumped on the box and knocked it over. He crawled out hesitantly and then, tail thumping maniacally, climbed on the boys to lick their laughing faces.

Lee guarded the infants in case the bigger puppy broke away. The gift included a crate, a sturdy pen, cleaning wipes, and a book on dog care and training the teenagers promised to read cover to cover. Overly excited, the puppy created a puddle the boys immediately cleaned up.

Lee handed his wife a smaller box. "Your idea for the puppy inspired me."

Jasirey removed the lid and lifted out a seal-point Himalayan Persian kitten that stretched, eyed her new surroundings, and ignored the four-times bigger ball of fur straining against human arms to reach her.

Scratching the tiny cat's chin, Jasirey sent her into a paroxysm of purring. The kitten resembled a miniature dust mop, so Jasirey named her Dusty. The teens named the dog Nick.

Christmas ended in thankful prayers with even the boys joining in.

❧ ❧ ❧

Jesse and Lill arrived the day prior to New Year's Eve for Jesse to examine his patients and for Lill to lend a hand with party preparations. The family invited the people. Whether on the same calendar day, the new year occasioned a celebration the various cultures had in common. Everett and Kharia planned refreshments.

More cunning each time Jesse saw them, the babies held their heads up and would soon be able to roll over. Jasirey had mostly healed.

"The pool is okay now," he said, "with maybe a week or two more before resuming your sex life. What option have you chosen for birth control?"

"I'll ask Liu to track my temperature and avoid sex during ovulation."

Not content to leave it to his patient's discretion—she seemed not the least invested—Jesse lobbed the ball into the husbands' court.

Fael, Ian, and Lee looked to Liu when asked for their birth control plan.

As Jesse suspected, they hadn't given it a thought. "Figure it out. Another pregnancy is inadvisable."

Lee asked, "How long between pregnancies do you recommend?"

"I don't advise another pregnancy," the doctor said, his gut beginning to gripe. "You're lucky she and the babies survived this one. It's unlikely she'd survive another."

129

The fathers' joy in their children had begun to mitigate the worry their gestation had wrought. Jasirey's vision quest prophesied an easier second pregnancy, and Jesse had said that anencephaly was rare. If necessary, they would camp at the hospital to prevent a replay of the quadruplets' birth.

"Jasirey is called to a higher and therefore protected purpose," Liu said.

Jesse's temper flared. "You call what that poor little thing suffered being protected?"

Lee glowered. "None of us would ever take away her choice."

"Just you wanting her to get pregnant again places great pressure on her."

"Normally, it is advised to wait one year before attempting pregnancy again," Liu said to the others, "though if her body cannot tolerate another, we shall bow to what must be."

As big a concession as he'd get, Jesse still hammered. "Take this into account. Facing another pregnancy frightens her."

Jesse nodded and went to find his wife.

The husbands consulted on what to do regarding theirs. Lee, Liu, and Fael expected Ian to be the most upset at Jasirey confiding her fears to the doctor rather than to her husbands.

On the contrary, he said, "In little more than ten months, our wife has become Jasirey, married four men practically strangers to her—"

"Ill through most of the marriage," Liu said.

"Has borne four infants," Fael said, "and endured the death of another."

Ian ran a hand over his head. "An overwhelming year. Perhaps we ought to allow Jasirey time to assimilate these changes before confronting and upsetting her."

Too fatigued to see any pitfalls in Ian's logic, the men agreed.

❧ ❧ ❧

Jasirey wore her new dress. It draped beautifully, hiding the small bulge left of the pregnancy belly. From nursing, her breasts rounded well above the neckline. She tried to adjust it and settled for wearing Liu's shawl.

Dusty, sporting a twenty-pound purr in a three-pound body, demanded attention. Jasirey scratched her ears and chin. They needed a cat tower to distract her from climbing the curtains. Duty called. Jasirey sighed, placed the kitten in her crate, and went downstairs.

Conversation in the living room halted as their lady entered. Everyone bowed. Ian swept her into a waltz. After a few turns, Lee claimed her, circled the room, and handed her to Fael. Liu followed and led her to a chair at music's end.

Jasirey's perspiring forehead and struggle for breath embarrassed her. Thankfully, the noise level resumed as she recovered.

Wearing a holly green sheath that showed her athletic figure to good advantage, Lill offered Jasirey a cup of punch. "Decorating took all my time today. We'll visit more tomorrow."

Jasirey smiled politely as Jesse and Ian approached. Jesse asked her to dance, and Ian unfurled a hand to Lill. The music flowed, a slow tempo. Jasirey relaxed into the swaying steps.

Jesse smiled fondly. "Where'd you go?"

"Oh, sorry. You dance so well, I floated along."

Jasirey managed another dance with each husband and one with Everett who, realizing she was overtaxed, walked her to the elevator.

"Go up," he said. "I'll inform your husbands. It's almost time for the fireworks."

She had opted to stay in with the babies. Hugging Everett in thanks, she went up to flop face down on the bed until Kimika woke her for the next feeding.

❋ ❋ ❋

A few weeks later, the babies' first real smiles enchanted their fathers and brothers. Watching that light much like their mother's on their tiny faces woke the husbands. There had been only perfunctory smiles from their wife in weeks and no sign of a returning libido.

In the training building, the teens confronted their stepfathers after the lesson. "Are you guys and my mom fighting?" Christopher said.

"We are not," Liu said. "Why do you ask?"

"You used to talk to each other and, you know, touch all the time."

"How come you stopped?" Michael's voice trembled.

Lee clutched the boy to him. Jasirey's vision of a break with her husbands after the babies' birth slashed through his mind.

Ian hugged Christopher. "Thank you for bringing this to our attention. I promise we'll take care of it."

131

After the boys returned to the house, Fael blasted a heavy exercise ball across the room with a side kick. "We failed to keep watch."

Liu placed his hands over his face, then took a deep breath and said, "Perhaps we could not have stopped the prophecy, but as you say, Fael, we should have remembered and watched for it."

That evening, Satoko and Mashita fed the little ones while the husbands set out the adults' dinner in the bedroom.

Ian seated Jasirey and came straight to the point. "We're worried, love. You don't seem yourself. Jesse said it's all right, yet you haven't used the pool."

"Time goes so quickly from one feeding to the next. It'll be longer soon."

It sounded reasonable, but the men recognized the excuse behind it.

"Precious one, has your libido not returned or do you fear pain or becoming pregnant?"

"You guys decide sex issues."

Dinner was not a resounding success.

❊ ❊ ❊

As she prepared for bed, Jasirey indulged a pouncing, stalking Dusty.

Lee gave the cat twenty minutes. "We've spoken to Master Kai," he said. "He's asked us to visit the island."

"Why?" Jasirey had no desire to travel with four babies and everything that went with them.

Fael cleared the tears clogging his throat and moved in to kiss her. She neither resisted nor responded.

"Fael, not tonight. I'm sorry."

"It is we who are sorry. We bungled our watch and missed the separation growing between us."

Jasirey shrugged. "I think that's inevitable, at least till newborns start sleeping through the night."

❊ ❊ ❊

The next morning, Jasirey heard the babies stirring and started to rise but couldn't budge the bodies entwined about her, a sleeping position the men hadn't used for some time and a surprise after her refusal to have sex the night before.

Lee reached for her as the babies started yelling. The adults groaned and got up to answer their summons.

132

Jasirey found it easier to concentrate on her babies' faces than to interpret the men's feelings. They petted her while caring for their children. She had expected them to be angry. Jasirey drifted as Safia nuzzled her way to the nipple. She laughed as her son Sun Li chortled and grabbed hold of Lee's dreadlocks.

Satoko and Mashita exchanged glances. After the feeding, they encouraged the men to bring Jasirey back to the bedroom for breakfast where Lee started a fire. Ian drew Jasirey to the sofa and onto his lap. Fael joined them to rub her feet.

"We haven't done this in a long time," Jasirey said.

Though wistful, her voice contained no note of blame or censure. Nonetheless, the words stung the husbands.

Jasirey trained her gaze on the fire. "When you say Kai asked us to go to the island, I assume he ordered it. Is this about what happened when I was kidnapped? I know you're all still angry."

"At what, precious one?" Liu asked.

"Not really sure," she mumbled. "For letting you down?"

"Little one, I think you slipped—fell?—through the cracks we made by not paying attention."

Jasirey sighed. Her teddy bear hadn't mixed up his metaphors in a while. "Please, let's not cast blame." She stowed the bitter thought that she had caused the mess behind shutters. "Maybe going to the island will help."

❇ ❇ ❇

On the island, the Imperiat and council deliberated on ways to best serve Jasirey's family.

The people naturally hoped to celebrate the anniversary of finding Jasirey and the birth of the babies. The Imperiat asked them to combine the parties after granting the family a week to acclimate.

Family members of the returning people and Master Kai greeted Ian's plane. A horse-drawn cart also waited.

Jasirey frowned at their attempt to coddle her. Then color suffused her face as her husbands set the infants, asleep in their carriers, into the cart meant more for them. Kai opened his arms to her. Jasirey respected decorum and kept the embrace brief.

He whispered, "Do not fret, dearest one," and assisted her into the cart next to her children.

133

The family had left New England with gloomy skies and freezing temperatures, and Jasirey had forgotten her sunglasses. The stinging heat raised the hairs on her exposed skin, though the sun's glare gave her a handy excuse to stare at the cart's floor.

The people knew the circumstances of the birth. Speculation filled the grapevine that their lady returned to introduce the babies and to heal, for they vividly remembered the prophecy of the sick light. Prayers for Jasirey filled the ether.

A house had been furnished for the family and included two bathrooms, a Western-style kitchen table, and the large bed from their honeymoon in the master bedroom. The family stayed in for their first evening.

In the cool of the morning, Christopher and Michael champed at the bit to go find friends. Their mother waved them off and smiled in surprise when they first hugged her of their own accord.

Also eager to introduce their expanded family, the dads each strapped an infant facing forward in a harness on his chest. Jasirey suggested she stay behind but immediately rescinded at Satoko and Mashita's shocked faces. She trailed the men to the marketplace.

The babies reached for every green leaf, every vivid flower, and bounced and beamed at the friendly faces milling about the village center.

Though trying to keep track of Jasirey in the throng, the men got caught up in being proud papas. The people drew their lady into their midst, bombarded her with questions—the babies' health, Michael and Christopher's schooling, the house and the people working there—and chipped away at her reticence.

After a while, the men remembered they had promised to take the teens to the training center late morning to combat jet lag and went to meet them at the school.

The people ensconced Jasirey and the infants in a nearby childcare center where caregivers changed diapers and held bottles. Jasirey left her little ones in their capable hands to return to the marketplace where she encountered a circling crowd who talked of life on the island the past year before easing into serious topics.

"We worried fearfully at your abduction and rejoiced at your swift recovery," a woman said.

Jasirey visibly curled inward. Handed a glass of cold tea, she sipped until she could compose herself. The words so long bottled up against her husbands' disapproval of how she'd handled being caught in the snare of a human trafficker became a torrent—the searing pain from the endless ride in Eric's van, the horrendous things he had said, and the harrowing decision to try and remove her babies from his hands by refusing to eat.

Jasirey's words choked off. Such anger pressed in on her from all sides she fought to breathe.

"Precious lady, if it would appease you," a man said, "I would gladly lay hands on that beast, even if for a few moments. You acted most courageously."

Certain they didn't understand her ironic attempt at self-protection that could have ended in her and the babies' deaths, Jasirey slowly raised her eyes. Only love and concern shone from the people's faces.

"I think he's dead," she blurted out.

The people cheered, and Jasirey couldn't help laughing, the laughter of lightness—not over a man's death, but from the joy the people's loving acceptance gave her.

❃ ❃ ❃

The council and Imperiat invited Jasirey and her husbands to the council hall the next day.

Invite, my butt, Jasirey thought. She didn't protest when they seated her husbands to the side with Master Kai. She held the usual cup of tea on her lap to hide her trembling. Lunar moths flapped in her stomach. The people's open-armed welcome bolstered her spirits. She feared the leader's reactions. Their sheer number further intimidated her.

"You recover from prolonged physical and an acute emotional trauma," Master N'yu-wen said. "We wish you to describe your experience, so we may better serve you."

Jasirey laid down the untouched tea. "I'm sure my husbands—" She took a breath and swallowed. "I hate being a disappointment to you."

"Why do you believe you are?"

"They don't scold, but I feel their anger, the disapproval."

The leaders conferred in low tones.

Jasirey buried her face in arms circling her knees.

A woman addressed the disturbed husbands. "Do you comprehend that our lady's retreat was a means of coping with circumstances impossible to control, a survival mechanism?"

"We made mistakes," Ian said. "She stopped turning to us. We failed to pursue it."

"You believe the separation between you to be of her design."

"They're upset," Jasirey said, "about my actions when captured. I didn't mean to turn away from them." She laid out her sins, a penitent at the altar. "I couldn't seem to stop myself."

"As to your abduction," a man said, "you protected your unborn children from a repugnant fate. Your misdeed, if any, lies in pricking your husbands' egos, questioning their ability to protect you, which logically they failed to do since you rested in enemy hands."

The men flinched.

Jasirey protested. "That wasn't their fault."

"Nor yours. You have no knowledge of the means at their disposal."

"A lack we intend to remedy." Master N'yu-wen sat rigidly erect. "You will tour our security facility to ease your anxiety for the safety of yourself and your family. We also propose to assist your husbands in comprehending your experience and the role they played in your withdrawal. Gentlemen, we have the means to induce a facsimile of the hormonal changes our lady suffered."

Jasirey bolted upright.

The leaders sitting around her startled as a percussive wave of heat sent them swaying backward. Several tried to claim Master Kai's attention, but his gaze remained on Jasirey.

"I don't think so," she said quietly, firmly. "Men aren't geared to go through that. What good comes from them suffering?"

"Gentlemen?" Master Kai challenged them.

Smarting from the remark about failing their wife, Ian's voice clipped out. "If it helps."

"It won't," Jasirey said. "Can't you see?" The council and Imperiat's reproach rested on her husbands. Jasirey's teeth clenched. "I forbid it."

"Let me be clear," Master Kai said, more to the husbands, who were slower on the uptake.

Master Kai might have found it amusing except for the critical stakes and Jasirey's disquiet. He knew she understood precisely what they intended.

"This is not a punishment," he said for her sake. "There will, however, be no second pregnancy unless your husbands fully understand the possible repercussions to you."

Jasirey's guilt outweighed irritation at the leaders' presumption. She couldn't stand putting her husbands through more stress than they already had suffered during a difficult pregnancy.

Master N'yu-wen said to the men, "We monitor the dosage. The effects are reversible, temporary, with no aftereffects other than a firsthand, albeit truncated, glimpse of your wife's experience."

"I want to understand, loved one," Fael said. He welcomed clarity regarding the genesis of their ruptured relationship and insight into a permanent solution. With an irate protectiveness and utter terror that stopped the breath in his lungs, she wrapped her arms around him and blasted through the empathic blocks he kept at full strength around the council and Imperiat.

"We're ready," Lee said. Not interested in the why of the matter, he desired only to restore their marriage to its previous closeness.

Master Kai drew Jasirey from the room. "Come, dearest one. They shall be returned to you in the morning." He linked hands to steady and comfort her.

After escorting Jasirey home and returning to the Imperiat domicile, Kai was informed of the incident with those who had been sitting around her during their meeting. Unsure how to harness her energy, he did recognize that strong emotions triggered spurts of growth in Jasirey's power.

The healer Niharu waited for Ian, Lee, Liu, and Fael in an enclosed room within the infirmary. Protectors stood guard outside the door. The intended medication, antidote, and restraints for safety lay on a table with buckets lined underneath.

Niharu considered the proceeding poetic justice. The men had left their lady unprotected. As a trainee Protector the previous year and therefore ineligible as a candidate for the husband ceremony, Niharu believed Jasirey would have fared far better had she had him at her side.

He hoped to be chosen as a possible future father for her next pregnancy, and considering events, perhaps she would even wish other husbands. Illness had caused her past rebuff of him. Niharu intended to change her mind.

He dispensed the oral medication, simulated hormones that would cause the husbands to experience some of Jasirey's physical symptoms, such as crawling ants, as well as the emotional ups and downs.

Niharu ordered the men to sit and meditate.

Jasirey's fear seared in his mind, Fael concentrated on warding off negative imaginings.

Ian expected the exercise to be a waste of time. He didn't believe anything could duplicate in the men what Jasirey had endured nor replicate her remarkable determination and courage. He also pushed aside the unworthy but persistent suspicion that Jasirey had inherited some measure of her mother's instability that may have worsened her suffering.

Shuddering at the taste, Lee swallowed the brew and focused on a prayer for his wife. The babies' well-being in large part depended on Jasirey's, as did his and the other husbands'. He closed his mind to worry.

Reality could at times punch the teeth out of theory, but Liu believed his training provided a realistic idea of what lay in store for them.

Fael felt the first stirring of something amiss and meditated to tamp it down. His focus scattered after a couple of hours as he fought nausea.

Master Kai entered silently to observe. Shooting a venomous glare at the healer, Ian rose to pace. Liu lunged for a bucket. Only Fael retained breakfast. Drenched in sweat, he rocked in misery. Lee surged to his feet and plowed a fist through the wall.

Niharu took a quick step behind Master Kai. The older man examined Lee as a tremor ran down the long length of his body.

Master Kai whispered, "Courage," and called in the Protectors.

By midafternoon, knowing they would be in misery as their stomachs rebelled against food, the men refused to eat. Liu felt guilty remembering all the meals he had insisted that Jasirey eat during her pregnancy.

The husbands paced or rocked to the point of exhaustion. At midnight, Master N'yu-wen administered a restorative herbal drink, and the men gratefully slid into oblivion.

Master Kai returned early in the morning. The men had not recovered sufficiently to face Jasirey.

He debated what to impart to them in their weakened state. The intensity of the men's symptoms shocked him, especially since they barely hinted at the greater suffering Jasirey had endured for months.

"The hormonal effects our lady experienced," he said, "came upon her gradually rather than in the space of hours."

The tense slash of Ian's mouth softened with the hope that what Jasirey suffered over months of pregnancy had not been as acute as what the men experienced in only a few hours.

"Your symptoms persisted barely a day," Master Kai continued. "Jasirey experienced few reprieves, day in and day out, for months. Nor did you contend with the pain the physical changes of pregnancy forced on her. As she said, you are not geared to withstand it."

Ian's recognition that his wife suffered even more than he had feared turned his insides into a watery, sloshing mess that threatened to erupt.

"Dearest God in heaven." A bucket rattled as Lee pulled it toward him.

Master Kai ordered a bland breakfast for the men. "Do you now perceive your part in Jasirey's retreat from you? You supported her during the pregnancy, but afterward, with the care of four infants, you became overwhelmed. You procrastinated in confronting and stemming the schism opening between you.

"Jasirey sensed your emotional withdrawal," continued Master Kai. "She already felt criticized and divided from you concerning her actions during the abduction and took your further withdrawal, even though from fatigue, as tacit permission to withdraw as well—a bad combination, yes?"

Lee pushed the bucket aside. "She used up her strength in service to us, and we hadn't the strength to stem the repercussions. I vow never again."

Master Kai nodded. "Her love for you and her children is her greatest strength and your love for her, her anchor. She cannot survive intact without it, nor will you without her. As the council and Imperiat advised you after the Imperiatu husband ceremony, the physical and emotional bonds between a Jasirey and her husbands go deeper than for the average human. Other than superficial partings, you lose the ability to tolerate emotional or physical separations.

"We believe Jasirey's lack of libido, as you labeled it," Master Kai went on, "resulted from the emotional distance between her and all of you rather than from lack of interest. She cannot tolerate physical intimacy without emotional closeness."

❦ ❦ ❦

Waiting in a small room at the Imperiat domicile, the men sat hunched in their seats, hands dangling loosely between their knees.

Master Kai had fetched Jasirey. He regretted the dark circles under her eyes and brittle movements, signs of a bad night.

Entering the room, she cried out. "You said they wouldn't be hurt."

Four disheveled heads jerked toward their wife. Master Kai retreated unnoticed.

Sensing their desperate need to connect and her burden of guilt lessened by the unconditional support and lack of judgment of the Devoted, Jasirey urged her husbands to surround her on the floor. One at a time, they joined with her face to face—an emotional imperative to mate, to be one—warm honeyed belonging flowed through their veins and suspended pain and regret.

Sprawled in a heap afterward, Fael rested his head on Jasirey's breast and described their experience at the infirmary, their mental and physical agitation, irritation, and even paranoia. While under the influence of the drug, both Lee and Ian had believed Niharu conspired to poison them. Meditation, training—nothing stopped the onslaught.

"Though I knew the rest of the team were beside me experiencing the same things," Fael said, "I felt disconnected from them and utterly alone."

"Yes," Jasirey sighed. "After the babies' birth, the worst of it for me— I believed my actions during the kidnapping killed our little girl."

Fael groaned. "No, loved one, no."

Misery clouded Ian's dark eyes. "Baby, can you forgive me?"

"Isn't it you who has to forgive me?"

"Please don't think that. I've been an ass. I suspected your . . . struggles were rooted in your family history of mental illness."

Jasirey rose and pulled on her dress. "You mean my weaknesses. People scolded my brother for giving in to nonsensical thoughts, as if he chose to be irrational or could control his subconscious. In the same breath, they'd tell him to take his meds. If you could descramble a damaged brain by willpower, why would you need medication?"

Jasirey opened the door. "Babies must be looking for lunch."

The icy burn of adrenaline scourged the men as they scrambled into their trousers.

Alerted by staff, Master Kai met the family in the foyer. His eyes crinkled at the men's distraught faces. "You expected instant resolution?"

"Stay. Talk to Kai," Jasirey said. She lacked the energy to deal with the men.

Master Kai kissed her cheeks. "Go."

He waved the husbands into an office. "What problem has arisen?"

Red streaks crept up Ian's pale face. "Mental illness runs in Jasirey's family. I thought perhaps . . . " He shrugged.

"No doubt the ignorant and prejudiced," Master Kai said, "have reacted unkindly toward Jasirey's family history of mental illness—something she could have allowed to shame and embarrass her. Yet, she speaks of her brother and mother with great love." Master Kai smiled. "If not occasional exasperation."

Lee relaxed his bunched fingers and addressed Ian. "But it's still a sore spot, especially when someone she loves reacts negatively. Why didn't you share your misgivings with us?"

"During my childhood," Ian said, "such things weren't discussed openly. My parents spoke in whispers of people unable to cope, burdens to their families."

Hot embers glowed in Fael's eyes. Liu's head wagged.

"Gentlemen," Master Kai said, "Communication skills, both between you and Jasirey and among each other, remain a priority for you to pursue at home, yes?" He waited for their nod of agreement before continuing. "Ian, for your sake and your family's, educate yourself on mental illness. Otherwise, consider Jasirey's justified anger at your attitude a distraction from the core problem. Jasirey believes her weaknesses, as she labels them, contributed to—perhaps even caused— your marital predicament, a type of false pride in her self-reliance, the unconscious notion that she primarily affects events.

"Rather than a skill, however," Kai continued, "her self-reliance is fed by fear of rejection or of having her trust betrayed. Your goal is to regain your wife's trust and help accustom her to reach out to you and the Devoted whenever the need arises."

The Goddess of Mercy

The husbands subtly introduced the practice of checking in on everyone's well-being during family prayer. Concentrated on her physical welfare the past year, the men realized they had wrapped their wife in a cocoon, kept her from physical exertion, and contributed to her lack of stamina.

The babies' feeding schedule prevented Jasirey from daily trips to the pond, so for exercise, her husbands invited her to the training center during the children's morning nap and gave her short lessons in self-defense. Jasirey showed a natural aptitude and hitherto unknown competitive streak.

One morning, Liu felt a tap from behind on his shoulder. He half turned to find no one there and ended up off balance. Jasirey knocked him on his butt and laughed in delight.

He goggled at her. "How did you . . . ?

She reached down to help him up. "Never turn your back on a Jasirey."

❀ ❀ ❀

As promised, Ian investigated several sources of information on mental illness. No cure existed for afflictions such as bipolar disorder or schizophrenia. Considering people's attitudes similar to his, the often unwieldy and intimidating insurance and medical establishments, and the imprecise science of whittling down an individual's diagnosis and treatment options, it no longer surprised him that some gave up or resorted to self-medicating. He better appreciated Jasirey's strength and tolerance for her mother.

❀ ❀ ❀

At the anniversary/welcome babies party, the youngsters eyed the colorful lamb kebabs and fruits like mango with bright eyes of brown, green, gold, and black.

Jasirey dreaded a mountain of baby gifts but received just four. Collaborating, the people constructed matching wooden rocking horses sporting wool manes and tails, leather saddles and reins, detachable seats to encase unsteady babies, and island scenery painted on the bodies— heirloom treasures. Jasirey hugged as many of the craftspeople as could reach her.

Entertainment began during the last of the sunlight. The babies were serenaded until they fell asleep in their carriers.

The people had conspired on Jasirey's anniversary present. They urged the husbands and their lady into a two-horse cart while Satoko and Mashita climbed into another alongside the sleeping infants. The people promised to escort the teenagers home later.

The carts separated along different paths. The adults' conveyance delivered them to the small cabin of their honeymoon.

"Someone shall collect your milk in the mornings," the driver told Jasirey, "and leave food for dinner in the late afternoons." He whispered something to her as he helped her from the cart.

Lee and Ian clasped arms under their wife's legs and carried her inside.

With a pat to her rear, Lee set her on her feet by the bathroom. She first scooted to the wardrobe as the men lit candles surrounding the bed.

Jasirey reappeared wearing the sheer robe from the Imperiatu. She glistened in the candlelight. Her eyes glowed with love and desire, a precious gift the men pledged to never again take for granted.

Despite the joyful occasion, emotions from the past months broke through. Ian pulled Jasirey to him and whispered, "I'm so sorry, baby, so stupid. Forgive me—"

Jasirey whipped around, tackled him to the bed, and kissed away his worry lines. "No more feeling bad. We were lost. Let's celebrate. We're finding our way again. You are my everything."

In two days alone, healing leaped forward for Jasirey and the men. One indelible thing stood out. The family's welfare literally depended on their strong connection.

❧ ❧ ❧

As Master N'yu-Wen had recommended, Lee and Fael escorted Jasirey on her tour of the Devoted's underground security facility built within a dormant volcano. The long elevator ride beneath the surface and the immensity of the complex emphasized the technical proficiency of the Devoted. The men stayed close and glowered at the many Protectors sending avid looks their wife's way.

Two-thirds of the group had retained their vows not to marry. They remembered Jasirey's words at the fealty ceremony and believed she might in future wish to have more husbands.

Jasirey noticed Lee's ferocious expression and tried to remain aloof. Unfortunately, the Protectors reminded her of adoring puppy dogs.

"Recruitment has slowed for the near term," Fael said, "but will pick up again as our little ones mature and require individual security."

"Current activity," Lee said, "centers on hot spots prone to instability and on certain people of interest."

Lee didn't specify, but Marcus popped into Jasirey's head.

A woman approached, bowed in apology, and asked the men to consult on one of their previous assignments. Lee and Fael chose an Elder to escort their wife. After they left, two young Protectors offered to relieve the older woman. The Elder had much to do and politely deferred to Jasirey. Recognizing the woman's desire to be elsewhere, Jasirey affably agreed.

Andwar, muscular in a non-bulky way and a dark brown hue, had grown up in Chicago. Chen, a lanky Asian who didn't specify his country of origin, spoke fluent English. They showed her a meeting room, its central focus a massive world map dotted with varicolored magnets that indicated different missions and people. The numbers staggered her.

Another large room clacked and buzzed with fingers on keyboards, voices speaking into headsets, too many desks and people to see clearly.

"This is the command center," Andwar said in hushed tones. "We monitor activities and relay orders from here for our global businesses as well as missions."

People nodded without stopping to bow. It didn't occur to Jasirey, nor did the young men think to inform her, that a good deal of the activity in the command center related directly to the safety of her family and friends in the US. The Protectors focused on an agenda closer to home.

Compelling rather than handsome, Chen offered his arm to lead Jasirey into a corridor. "Perhaps you'd care for lunch before your husbands return."

She had expected to be shown more but, assuming the young men had duties to attend to, acquiesced. The cafeteria was equally spacious and full of diners who bowed to Jasirey. Not wanting to interrupt their meal, she found an empty table while Chen fetched a tray for her.

Andwar had an engaging smile. "The attention bothers you."

Jasirey shrugged and thanked Chen for a plate of rice, vegetables, and grilled white fish.

Three other men asked if they might join the group. Andwar introduced Nikolai, Favian, and Sajan, their eager young faces wreathed in smiles.

Jasirey carefully set down her fork—five men of different races. "They had no right," she gritted out. "It's too soon for the second pregnancy." She knew Kai and the Imperiat believed other men besides her husbands would father the next pregnancy, but fury built that they would orchestrate a meeting of candidates without consulting her.

Fearing she might bolt, Andwar laid a light hand on her arm and immediately retreated as burning pain singed his fingertips. He held up his hands in surrender. "Please, lady, we didn't mean to upset you."

"We meant only to introduce ourselves," Nikolai said. His bright idea to waylay Jasirey on her tour, he assumed responsibility.

Jasirey grudgingly met remorseful bright blue eyes. "I suppose you're all Protectors."

"I am afraid we have made an unfortunate error in judgment." Sajan's aquiline features formed a mournful cast. From India, he spoke English with a British accent. His natural charisma fizzled at seeing tears pool in their lady's eyes. "The Imperiat offered the Protectors a release from their vows. Many opted to remain in your service. We wanted to introduce ourselves ahead of the pack. I humbly beg your pardon."

"We blew it," Andwar said.

Favian's perfect Latin face mirrored the pain they had caused their lady. "The Imperiat may drum us out of the Protectors."

"The Imperiat didn't orchestrate this?" Jasirey asked.

"No, lady." Chen swallowed hard as her smile transformed her face.

They were all young—in their twenties, Jasirey guessed. "You've probably heard some of what we've been through."

As her Protectors, they were privy to a great deal of information and realized they had used it with brazen and childish intent. Sworn to protect and care for her, they had hurt her instead.

"You've behaved inappropriately."

Despite her mild tone, the men winced. The color of blue spruce trees, her eyes lit with an intriguing spark of humor.

"I won't tell if you don't."

The men gaped.

"Seriously, if word of this reaches my husbands, they'll pulverize you." The spark blazed and mesmerized the men, so that for the moment they forgot to feel awful about hurting her, even when she sternly said, "Go away."

Andwar bowed and saluted. "Thank you, Jasirey."

"Yes," Favian said. "Thank you for your kindness." He beamed a winning smile and instantly dimmed it at her coolly raised brow.

The young men saluted and scurried for the door. *Schmucks.* Jasirey's small smirk bloomed to full-fledged glee as the men practically bowled over Master Kai.

They stiffened to attention. Kai commanded their gaze for what must have felt like an interminable few seconds and then dismissed them.

He crossed to Jasirey. Though shadows filled her eyes, they also contained hints of humor. He hid his vast relief. *Fools.*

"No harm done?" he asked.

Jasirey burst out laughing but smothered it so as not to draw attention. "I think they learned their lesson. Don't be hard on them."

Master Kai considered that an interesting response.

Jasirey propped an elbow on the table, chin on her hand. "Who tipped you off?"

"The woman they involved in pulling away Fael and Lee. She realized the case in question had been closed and became suspicious of the young men's intentions."

Jasirey straightened. "Did she tell my husbands?"

"Concerned for Andwar and Chen's safety, she contacted me and presented another case to cover the Protectors' perfidy."

"That's good." Jasirey sighed. "I thought at first the Imperiat ordered the introduction."

Master Kai's eyes glinted. "Such a betrayal would have caused you great distress."

"Yes, but now I feel bad I thought that."

"Foolish child." Kai rose to replace her cold meal and returned along with Fael and Lee.

"Sorry for the interruption," Lee said. "You saw everything?"

"Tell them of your adventure," Master Kai said.

Jasirey mutely appealed to the older man.

He patted her hand. "Better family dynamics require better communication, yes?"

Lee rested his arm over Jasirey's shoulders with most of the weight on the back of the chair. "What happened?"

"Some Protectors decided to introduce themselves—five of them."

Lee's arm remained gentle, his expression not so much. Jasirey's vulnerability raised every protective instinct in her husbands, hypersensitive after failing her themselves. Lee envisioned wiping the floor with the interlopers.

"Did they hurt you?" Though asked in a calm tone, Fael's question demanded an answer.

"It hurt when I believed the Imperiat planned it. They admitted to acting on their own. Then I just thought, 'dumb putzes.' They left, tails tucked between their legs."

Master Kai snorted an undignified laugh and set Jasirey off.

Profoundly grateful for the return of their wife's feistiness, Fael and Lee joined in on the laughter.

❧ ❧ ❧

The Imperiat ordered the five rash Protectors to the Imperiat domicile. Leader of the team and several years older than the others, Nikolai led Andwar, Chen, Favian, and Sajan into the assigned, empty room and sat in one of five folding chairs placed before a table. Their leaders kept them waiting. The men came to attention as fifteen ranking members, faces impassive, filed in. Tea was not offered.

"As Protectors of Jasirey," a woman said, "you received private information regarding the physical and emotional trauma our most precious lady endured, a sacred trust you saw fit to violate."

Though delivered in quiet tones, the words lashed the already sore hearts of the young men.

"Your unauthorized actions might have caused grave consequences to her recovery. Especially you, Nikolai. You are close to infiltrating the trafficker Marcus's organization, a proven threat to our lady. Had you no concern for her welfare or that her trust in this body and therefore her willingness to accept assistance from us might be impaired?"

The men blanched. Nikolai's voice barely carried. "I'd give anything to undo my stupidity."

"We all agreed introducing ourselves before other Protectors was brilliant," Sajan said. He would not allow Nikolai to assume sole blame.

Elbows on his knees, Andwar wrung his hands. "We hoped to leave a good impression."

Chen sat ramrod straight. "Arrogant and self-centered."

"Now she will remember us with disdain," Favian said.

Perhaps sufficient atonement from the young men, they indicated a greater regret for Jasirey's reaction than for any punishment the Imperiat might impose.

Master Kai took a moment to calculate. "Our lady asked us to be lenient."

The men's heads whipped up in such hope that he had a difficult moment as he remembered Jasirey's imagery of tails tucked between their legs. He coughed to disguise a most inappropriate laugh. The young men did indeed resemble misbehaving puppies begging for forgiveness.

"Jasirey initiates and chooses," a man of the Imperiat said. "Forget that again, and we will divest you of your mandate as Protectors. Understood?"

Not taking the Imperiat's largess lightly nor Jasirey's, the young men rose and bowed.

Master Kai ended the interview. "She likes you. Do nothing to jeopardize that. Nikolai, a word, please."

Bowing repeatedly, their faces shining in gratitude for the conditional encouragement, the younger four men bounced out the door.

"Was that wise?" a woman asked Kai. "You believe Jasirey might yet consider them?"

"She wished to protect them. In the end, I believe she was amused and attracted."

Nikolai rose as Master Kai approached. The older man waved him back to his seat and sat beside him. "It is not like you to make such rash decisions, Nikolai. Tell me what you were thinking."

Nikolai scrubbed at his face with both hands. "I felt an overwhelming wish . . . no, need to be close to her." His head wagged. "I know all Protectors say the same. I have no excuse."

"I do not look for an excuse. I wonder if your work on the trafficking organization has you more worried for her safety than most."

"On missions, I have seen the cruelty and callousness people unleash on one another. The trail of human debris Marcus leaves behind stuns me. The thought of him getting his hands on her . . ."

Both men looked away. There was nothing more to say.

❧ ❧ ❧

Having discussed individual dates, Liu had drawn the highest card, and that evening after the babies had been put to bed, he pulled Jasirey against his body for a kiss. Since he seemed loath to come up for air, the others laughed and went for a walk.

Liu nibbled on his wife's ear and whispered, "Are they gone?" It tickled, and she giggled. He wormed his hands under her panties to cup her derriere.

"We should move this to the bedroom," she murmured.

On their bed, Jasirey fingered Liu's downy hair, imagining it grown long and Liu as a samurai warrior.

"Why are you snickering?"

Not realizing she was, she laughed and kissed the top of his head. "I pictured you in shoulder-length hair and a samurai outfit. Yes, I know that's Japan, but it's sexy."

His eyes sparkled in amusement. "Is it?"

"A bit of the conqueror peeks out of you. Very sexy."

Not sure at first about the conqueror bit, Liu decided to be flattered and smiled contentedly.

Jasirey became quiet, but he knew she remained awake.

She propped herself up on her elbow to look into his eyes. "Liu, you really accept a relationship between other men and Jasirey?"

A strange way to phrase it, Liu thought. He realized his wife remained ambivalent concerning her destiny and sought distance. "Shall I tell you how I see you in my imagination?" he asked.

"I'm all ears."

Liu knew that idiom from Lee. "Kuan Yin, the Goddess of Mercy, her name means: one who hears the cries of the world. On her way to Heaven, she heard an anguished cry from the earth and stopped to help.

As patron saint of Tibetan Buddhism, Goddess of mothers, and protector of all peoples, her image—usually a mother with a child in her arms—can be found throughout China in temples, dwellings, and some public places. When called upon, she can protect one's physical body and purify a heart of evil."

Jasirey blinked a moment. "Those gifts would come in handy."

Liu could not help laughing. "One day, my precious one, when you have fully come into your destiny, I shall remind you of this conversation."

❧ ❧ ❧

The next evening, Lee grabbed Jasirey's hand and drew her outside for a date but kept his plans a mystery. He led her in no discernible direction. Then she smelled salt water. Forest gave way to a starlit, rocky shore and a calm harbor. They picked their way to a dock for small craft. Lee boarded a sailboat not much bigger than a dinghy with a practiced bound and assisted her to a seat near the tiller.

Lee's muscles bunched and stretched as he rowed into the harbor. He hoisted a sail that immediately caught the wind. The boat glided into open water on moon-washed swells. Kneeling between Lee's legs, Jasirey pressed her cheek into his shoulder to stay warm against the brisk wind.

Lee knew he would remember the evening as one of his happiest times with her and marveled anew that she had chosen him. The love, affection, and heady passion his wife showered on him overwhelmed him at times. After an hour, he steered to a sheltered cove, lowered the sail, and dropped anchor.

Jasirey's glittering eyes sent Lee's pulse pounding. She molded her body to his, slanted her lips softly over his, and untied his tunic. Her nails lightly raked his chest, and the heat of her mouth followed their trail. He became lightheaded as his oxygen and blood supply rushed downward.

151

Unable to physically budge him, she pulled at his trousers until he got the idea and lifted his hips. She pushed his trousers down, then toppled him onto some cushions.

She wriggled between his legs to part them and said, "My own personal mast."

Her delectable mouth latched on and almost demolished Lee's control. Jasirey could undo her men in minutes but had learned to prolong their pleasure. Her tongue and enveloping mouth hurled Lee wave over wave, the height nearly unbearable.

He raised himself to grasp her hips and swung her lower body toward him. Jasirey continued her ministrations throughout the swivel. To hell with the niceties. He tore away the crotch of her damp underwear and hunched forward. Sometimes being tall was a hindrance. She tasted heavenly, which distracted him long enough to prod her into a strong orgasm. He gripped his wife's hips and shattered into a kaleidoscope of brilliant shards.

While cuddling afterward, Jasirey reluctantly pointed to wet spots darkening the bodice of her dress through leakage pads. "Babies are calling."

Lee's fingertip tested the dampness. "I could help." His dimples appeared as his head leaned forward to join his finger.

Jasirey swatted his hand. "Shame on you, stealing from babies. I'm telling."

Lee dragged her across his lap and gently spanked her behind over what was left of her underwear.

❧ ❧ ❧

Neither Ian nor Fael received their date. Kharia called from America. Jasirey's mother had suffered a heart attack. No serious damage, but with reduced heart function from previous infarctions, the long-term prognosis was worrying.

Ian arranged to go home first thing in the morning.

Jasirey gazed at Lee, Liu, and Fael. "I hate not being able to acknowledge you guys or our beautiful babies to my family."

"Married an entire year," Fael said, "and we seldom consider the cost to you, restrained from disclosing details of your life to family and friends. Are we—our life together—sufficient?"

"You guys are my life. I'll never regret choosing us. If others want to be sucky, let 'em." She made a face. "You'll have to call me Shannon. Hope I remember to answer to it." Her lips parted in an unconscious invitation. "It'll be hands off and no combustible looks."

"Perhaps if you refrained," Lee said, "we'd manage more easily."

"Suck it up."

"Stop saying that," Ian growled. The impish light in her eyes did it. He disposed of her nightshirt and nuzzled a softly heavy breast. The others joined in the playfulness, released regrets, and gave and received all the acceptance and belonging they needed.

❧ ❧ ❧

Master Kai saw the family off and embraced Jasirey for a long moment. "Always remember, dearest one, we are here for you."

The family finalized their plans on the plane. With no idea how long the visit to her parents' home in South Carolina would last, Jasirey vetoed the idea of expressing her milk. They'd bring all the kids.

They stopped overnight in western Massachusetts to pick up Kimika and a security force adequate to ensure the children's safety. Robin would come as the family's driver.

Jasirey called her parent's house, and Natalie answered. Their mother's doctor had scheduled her to return home in the morning. Natalie stated pointblank that the house contained no room for Shannon, Ian, and the boys.

"No, of course not. We've booked a hotel."

"Nice, if you can afford it."

When Jasirey ended the call, Lee searched her face. "That was short."

"Natalie's a little miffed we have money for a hotel."

Lee dropped the subject. Natalie was his least favorite in-law.

All the kids were cranky in the morning. Their mother understood perfectly. After a short trip to South Carolina, Fael, Liu, Kimika, and his people accompanied the children to the hotel while Robin drove Ian, Lee, and Jasirey to her parents' home forty miles from the airport.

Anne and Richard owned a suburban ranch house. A pinched expression on her face, Natalie answered the door.

Jasirey received a perfunctory hug and entered directly into the living room. Bundled in blankets despite the mild day, Anne rested on a recliner.

"How are you, Mom?" Jasirey asked.

"I'm fine. You can't believe a word those doctors say. We have good insurance, so they order tons of tests and prescriptions to make money."

Jasirey resisted arguing against the old refrain.

Anne shifted fretfully. "You haven't visited me since the wedding. It's not like you can't afford the travel expenses." She glared at Ian.

Jasirey perched on the chair arm to hug her mother. "Building the house, school for the boys—I'll do better this year. I've missed you."

Coming in from the kitchen, Richard offered coffee or iced tea.

Jasirey rose to hug him. "Mom, be right back. I'll help Dad serve the drinks. Where's Marcie?" she asked her father.

"At the store buying extra steak. You know your mother's not happy unless she's feeding people." He recounted what the doctors told them and explained that they'd scheduled Anne's original appointment for a urinary tract infection. "She had a series of small heart attacks she didn't even feel. The bypass from fifteen years ago has held. The two arteries they couldn't fix are worse. They put her on a blood thinner. Not much else they can do, but she's a tough old bird."

"Mom," Jasirey said on returning to the living room, "we're not staying to eat. We can bring takeout tomorrow when Michael and Christopher come. The traveling wore them out today."

Anne's argument got cut off as Marcie returned and gave Jasirey a tight hug and Ian a friendly one.

The sisters had little in common physically. Ian and Lee naturally thought Jasirey was the loveliest, though Marcie possessed the more attractive features. Jasirey's beauty resided in her expressive warmth. Fit and happy, only her silver hair advertised her as the eldest sibling, which infuriated Natalie.

"Some people have all the luck," she said. "You throw away a career to be a housewife and still land on easy street."

"I threw away nothing. I chose motherhood, my best destiny."

"And a waste of education," Anne said. "All those brains, college, and nothing to show for it. Doesn't it bother you you never accomplished anything?"

Once crushed by such remarks, Jasirey merely said, "Depends on your definition of accomplishment."

"Marcie's a mother," Natalie said. "She didn't use it as an excuse to stop working."

Marcie stole a glance at Ian. He and the large, steely-eyed bodyguard, Lee, remained silent, their mouths hard slashes. She shrugged at Jasirey, the sister she knew only as Shannon.

Marcie had not gone to a casino or bought a scratch ticket in almost a year and blessed her sister for insisting she get treatment. Shannon didn't spare her the truths she needed to hear but never put her down and, miraculous to Marcie, stopped Paul's belittling. Neither her husband nor sister volunteered what passed between them. Grateful for Paul's forbearance, Marcie didn't dig.

❧ ❧ ❧

The next day, Fael opted to be included in visiting Jasirey's parents.

Anne ignored Fael in the excitement of welcoming her two tall, handsome grandsons.

They described their schooling—Natalie considered the curriculum odd—their friends and their martial-arts training.

Their grandmother wrinkled her nose. "Kirani and Bazir—they sound foreign."

Christopher's jaw set. "Their father's Irish, their mom's Turkish. They're nice."

"Arabs." Natalie eyed Fael. "Are you crazy, letting terrorists into your house?"

Not necessarily agreeing with her vocal younger sister, Marcie stayed silent. But really, Shannon should know better than to bring a person such as Fael to their parents' house.

Jasirey's sons had experienced their relatives' limited views on other cultures before, but Jasirey refused to subject them to further diatribes. "We brought chicken marsala," she said, "and stuffed tilapia."

Anne joined the adults in the dining room. The boys sat to the side behind TV trays. Jasirey insisted Fael be included at the main table.

Marcie recounted her daughter's accomplishments, a safe dinner topic. Born between Christopher and Michael, her schedule resembled her parents'—chock full of school, church, and charitable functions.

Jasirey likened the nonstop activity to binge eating. Stuff yourself full to push down all the pesky thoughts and feelings that pained you.

"Your Uncle James is giving a party this weekend," Anne said. "I told him you'd be there."

"Mom, we haven't decided how long we're staying."

"He expects you. Is it asking too much for you to spend time with your family?" She turned suspicious eyes on Ian, though James knew him and said he was a respected businessman. Anne placed a lot of store in her brother's opinion. He was a successful man.

Mother's guilt—Jasirey usually allowed it to roll off but couldn't justify aggravating a sick woman. She filled the dishwasher and called it a night.

Returning to the hotel, the family conducted prayers. Jasirey let the others tuck the babies into bed and drew a quiet Fael into the bedroom while Ian filled in Liu and Lee.

Ian suspected Fael was perturbed by the toxic spewing during the visit. He trusted their wife to sort him out.

Jasirey circled Fael's waist and rested her head on his shoulder. He clamped his arms around her like a vice. "My Fael, I suppose you lowered your blocks to get an unadorned experience of my family. I'm good at tuning them out." She added the last in the assumption his grim unease stemmed from concern for her.

Fael searched her clear eyes filled with sympathy and a twinkle of humor. "What amuses you?"

"The human condition, laugh or be swamped. I forgot that for a while. I won't again."

"I believe you, loved one." Her smile bathed him in warm acceptance and hot need.

She twined fingers through his thick hair and pulled him into a kiss meant to comfort by numbing his brain. Their bodies joined, slapping together in frantic rhythm to a teeth-clenching climax.

Fael collapsed and laughed raggedly into his wife's damp neck. "I feel much better now, my beloved."

Revered Vessel

The next day, Anne patted Ian's hand as he agreed to attend the party. When he asked about his security attending, she said, "It's the more-the-merrier type of affair."

Anne doubted her sister and two brothers would dare object to the foreigners since some of their own children married outside their race and gave them dark grandchildren. Anne didn't understand it, but the world had changed and become a scary place, full of murder and mayhem. She didn't dare wear her jewelry in public anymore.

Neither of Jasirey's sisters could miss more work to attend the party. Natalie bent a bit, hugged Jasirey goodbye, and pecked Ian on the cheek.

Marcie hugged him. "Shannon's happier. I'm glad she found you." Ian kissed her cheek.

The rest of the week, Anne talked incessantly about the upcoming gathering and her siblings. None of them had as beautiful a daughter or one who married so well or had the money for island vacations and personal security guards.

Jasirey recognized the futility of enlisting her father to prevent her mom from going on a cooking spree for the party.

He refused to put himself in harm's way, so Jasirey, Michael, and Christopher spent several hours helping Anne bake cookies and enjoyed the time together.

Jasirey also knew wearing one of her comfortable island dresses would precipitate a loud fit. She had brought a blouse and a pair of slacks she hoped would do.

As the men and the boys had packed only shorts and T-shirts, Ian took them shopping. On their return, they handed a glittery box to Jasirey. Her surprised delight rewarded their effort. Inside lay a black, V-neck cocktail dress. Bold sweeps of blue, purple, and green adorned the skirt and reminded Jasirey of the colored beads the Devoted included at the waist of all the dresses they had made for her when she visited the island. A filmy swirl of black met at the conservative neckline and flowed past the shoulders to a low V in the back. The line of the dress subtly accentuated her curves.

"I found the dress," Christopher said.

Michael handed her black sandals with dark purple stones on top. "I found these."

The night of the party, all her husbands looked handsome in black trousers and jewel-toned shirts that matched the colors in her skirt.

Her white lion guarded the babies. Jasirey hugged him. "I know I'm leaving them in the best of hands."

Kimika smiled fondly. "And yet you cannot help worrying. I won't leave their sides."

❧ ❧ ❧

Jasirey's uncle owned a large house in an affluent neighborhood. People crammed both the house and deck. A paunchy man, James bussed his niece's cheeks with loud smacks and shook her well-connected husband's hand two-handed. Latching onto the attractive couple's arms, he dragged them from one business comrade to another.

Anne and Richard arrived, a good excuse for Jasirey to escape her uncle. She greeted her parents, her mother's sister Marion, and Marion's kids. Jasirey hadn't met one cousin's wife or their two children. The wife's parents visited from India and attended with them. Jasirey extended her hand to the older couple. They stared at Jasirey's bracelet, their eyes widened in shocked recognition, and they bowed.

Jasirey stepped closer to cover their reaction. "Please, not here," she whispered. "It's safer for my family to remain anonymous. Can you understand?"

Watching over Jasirey, Lee and Fael adroitly steered the couple aside.

Marion sidled up to her favorite niece who always had a hug for her aunts and uncles. Not sure why, she lowered her voice. "Everything all right?"

Jasirey raised her hand. "They recognized my bracelet. It's a historic piece."

As a child, Jasirey had begged Marion to share her knowledge of rocks and minerals whenever the families visited and had received her first bracelet of polished stones from her.

158

"Oh, that's beautiful. From your husband?"

Jasirey smiled. "Handed down from his family." She chatted for a bit, then went to check on her sons. They and cousins somewhere on the family tree had formed a mini party in the game room.

Corporate types surrounded Ian to talk shop. He caught her eye and winked, but she knew he felt besieged and waded in. "Excuse us, gentlemen, I need to introduce Ian to several family members."

Ian took her arm. "Thank you," he whispered. "I appreciate the rescue."

Collecting her other three husbands along the way, Jasirey led them to the deck. The house had become warm and stuffy. It would get chilly before long, but for the time being, the coolness cleared her head and relieved a stress headache.

It required a lot of mental energy for an introvert to be sociable in a throng of people. Of her husbands, Fael alone experienced the same thing, but believed by the hosts and guests to be an employee, he wasn't expected to interact.

"Did we scare that poor couple who recognized my bracelet?" Jasirey asked Lee.

"They understood and agreed not to discuss the Devoted with anyone."

"How did they know about the bracelet and Jasirey?"

"The wife has a brother who is a farmer on the island," Fael said. "He had clearance to give broad details to the couple and enlist them in trade with the Devoted."

"We need to remind him," Lee said, "that discussing Jasirey is off limits."

Lee's flexing bicep left no doubt that it would be a forceful reminder.

Jasirey patted Lee's arm and walked back inside to brave the crowd at the bathroom where a line of chatting women waited. She wandered into a sunroom she'd been in before. It included a protected wall of family photos. She loved the picture of her grandparents' 1920s wedding. In a fascinating clash with the staid woman Jasirey remembered, her grandmother wore a white-lace, knee-length flapper's dress.

A shadow fell on the picture. She glanced behind her and froze as old alarms pealed. A shock of white-blond hair and pale eyes wavered in Jasirey's dimming vision. She fought to turn through the muffling white noise in her head. *Breathe—concentrate. Not elderly. Medium height, bulky—breathe.*

"Such panic, I believe I'm honored." A feral light sparked in the eerie eyes of Marcus without the disguising green contacts and drab brown wig he'd worn when accosting Jasirey in the dress shop the previous year.

In her mind, Jasirey saw a rabid nest of roiling emotions buried beneath Marcus's cultivated surface of icy detachment that fed on others' heightened emotions, the one thing able to bore through the ice.

"What can I do for you?" she asked with perfect calm, her only armor.

"Admirable recovery, ducky. Tell me, your four bastards—no, one or more may be legitimate. What do you suppose is the going rate for Jasirey's progeny?"

Her eyes flashed.

Marcus's breath quickened as he fought an undeniable urge to step back from her. "Ducky doesn't quite suit you, does it? Highness—yes, much better. No answer? No matter. I don't mind a bit of research."

The man loomed closer. Jasirey jabbed hard at his Adam's apple and sprinted for the door. Thick fingers wrapped around her neck and jerked her against his chest. Her body instinctively stilled. Quieting the gonging alarm in her head took more effort.

"I harbor no resentment toward you, highness. I do wonder to what degree damage inflicted on you or your children will affect your men. That interests me greatly."

Damp lips grazed Jasirey's ear. She brutally quelled the bile welling up.

"Tell Ian my magnanimous frame of mind has a short shelf life. Now, you'll want to hurry to your brood, won't you?" He lightly squeezed her neck and released her.

Jasirey fled, terrified as she pictured slimy covetous feelers reaching for her.

Lee waited outside the bathroom and rushed to his panic-stricken wife. He half carried her back to the others on the more private deck.

"Lee, stop. The babies, he's going after them. Call Kimika. Warn him."

Lee grabbed his phone. Fael steadied Jasirey's heaving shoulders. "Who?"

"Marcus." Fael whipped around. "He'll be gone," she said to empty space. Marcus certainly wouldn't hang around.

"No answer." Lee tucked Jasirey to his side and forged through the crowd.

Ian gave hasty farewells and ordered Liu to gather the boys.

Robin at the wheel, the limo waited at the entrance with Fael, his gold eyes flat and hard. Jasirey sat between her sons and kept a tight grip on their hands while Lee and Ian punched phone numbers to no avail.

Christopher eyed Ian. "What's happening?"

Michael raised his free fingers to his mouth but lowered them to cover his mother's hand that clutched his.

"A threat to your brothers and sisters," Ian said. "Don't worry. Kimika's there."

Besides Robin, one security woman had accompanied the family. The harried men wanted Jasirey and the boys far from the danger Marcus posed.

Fael cradled her face. "You cannot help. Let Robin remove you, Michael, and Christopher from harm's way. Go to the airport. My word, we will follow with the babies."

Robin nodded at Fael in the rearview mirror.

His partner surveyed the road behind them. "No one following," she said.

Robin sped for the hotel and soon screeched to a halt in front. The men grabbed guns from a locked cabinet and flew through the entrance.

Jasirey's gaze became unfocused as a memory washed over her. She'd asked Master Kai if a white lion had been at the husband ceremony in the Imperiatu. He'd assured her only men but to hold the strong vision close. Her white lion would never allow anyone to harm her babies.

Her body stiffened as realization dawned. A brief image flared of large SUVs boxing in their car and forcing it off the road. She was Marcus's target. She had no time to waste questioning how she knew. She acted.

"Everyone out. Get my sons inside."

Jasirey made a production of slamming her door and ran for the highway.

Clueless as to what their lady intended, Robin ordered his partner to take charge of the teenagers and followed Jasirey. Two black-clad figures glided past his line of vision. He never saw the third.

Jasirey chanced a glance behind her and saw Robin following, slinking shadows, and the security woman hustling the boys into the hotel.

Robin stumbled and fell. *Oh, God.*

She reached the road and hesitated in the face of oncoming traffic. Lightning bolts sizzled through her as she crumpled into a ball of twitching muscles. One of the shadows bent close. She felt a sharp pain in her buttock and was swallowed by darkness.

❧ ❧ ❧

Aboard his merchantman, Marcus brushed his dogs' teeth. His mind roamed to the sturdy form of Jasirey. Excellent stock. Marcus planned to obtain the offspring later. Four, what a lovely surprise that news had been. A flash of excitement left goose bumps on his skin as he thought about how he might persuade Jasirey to help him acquire her children.

He anticipated Ian, Lee, Liu, and Fael's time-consuming search for their squalling progeny and their sleepless nights envisioning but never knowing the children's fate. That lack of closure would be Marcus's exquisitely torturous revenge.

Strafe's report said the men cared for the woman, a bonus of pain for them. Speaking truthfully, Marcus did not seek direct revenge on her, though after their encounter in the dress shop, he often imagined bending that remarkable will to his.

❧ ❧ ❧

Two of Marcus's men carried the inert body of the woman he had sent them to procure down a passageway of the ship. Familiar with their boss's eccentric ways, they said nothing when an African crewman swabbing the floor insisted on wresting her from them. Shrugging, they took up their post outside the door of her cubicle. Marcus wanted the bitch in his stateroom as soon as she woke.

Reeling from shock, Mtombe carried Jasirey into the metal-walled room and gently laid her on a narrow cot. Mtombe had not seen Jasirey since the Imperiatu, the test that decided she was actually Jasirey, and the ceremony where she chose her husbands. Among the candidates, Mtombe had realized he didn't belong on the island, and she had freed

162

him from his vows as a Protector to go and find the path meant for him. He had happily embraced a new path though he had been thrilled to hear about the birth of her four babies.

Now here she was, back in his life. He covered her with a thin blanket while wracking his brain for a plan. He must first protect her and second, free her—an impossible feat alone and without backup.

❦ ❦ ❦

Kimika's team reported that the mercenaries Marcus sent to the hotel fled after capturing Jasirey, clearly their goal since they never entered the hotel. He set up his computer and traced her embedded tracking device until it stopped at the Columbus Street Terminal of Charleston Harbor and gave him the coordinates of Marcus's merchantman.

Kimika and the husbands feared Marcus's reaction if they tried to infiltrate the ship. They couldn't take the chance he might kill Jasirey.

They contacted the Imperiat who sent Nikolai and his team: Andwar, Chen, Favian, and Sajan. Nikolai started making enquiries into a meeting with Marcus the minute their plane reached altitude, using the name Iurii that he had assumed when assigned the mission to court the trafficker into doing business with him as an import/export businessman.

Fixing impassivity on his face, he waded through Marcus's minions. A man capable of connecting Nikolai directly to Marcus eventually came onscreen.

"Whaddya want?"

"Someone who can get it for me. You have their whore on the ship. If I know this, Ian and his men soon will." A not so veiled threat.

Marcus left him waiting. "Iurii, what can I do for you?"

"Ask what I can do for you."

Marcus remained unmoved.

"I know you hold Jasirey. She's no good for the markets you deal in. I've associates of the superstitious sort to whom her whelps are worth a great deal."

"And what brings you to the conclusion that I have this woman?"

Not deceived by the man's calm voice, Nikolai launched into a semblance of the truth to appease Marcus's anger at the implied breach to his security. "You well know I haven't the resources to pull off your

163

bold play. I'm told she's still fertile. I'll breed her until her body gives out, then sell her." Feeling his leaden facial muscles cramp, Nikolai still managed a shark's smile. "Perhaps back to her men."

Marcus's strange eyes flared. "Be interesting to see if they'd take her. State your offer."

"A lump sum for the bitch, a share for each pup."

"Going to father them yourself?" The eyes glittered.

Nikolai had no need to feign disgust. "Hardly. I'll leave that dubious pleasure to my men."

"I've no interest in a long-term deal." Not averse to giving up his prize, Marcus never allowed pleasure to override business, and Nikolai's knowledge of her worth posited him as a person to exploit for information hard to come by on the name Jasirey.

The younger man's open-mouthed response to the price he named amused Marcus. "I will of course interrogate her first."

Nikolai held a small ray of hope that the man had not yet touched Jasirey. He allowed a whine to creep into his voice. "She's no good to me too ill-used to breed, and my customers will perceive defects in the mother as a sign of defects in the offspring, bad for business."

Marcus's lips curled. "A sound body it is."

❄ ❄ ❄

Cold, aching muscles forced Jasirey back to consciousness. Cramps spiked in her stomach, and a recessed fluorescent bulb glared into her eyes. Squinting to look around, she saw a metal toilet, slowly forced her body up to use it, then curled back up on the cot.

A soft knock barely gave her warning before a man entered. The harsh light cast bluish tints onto his ebony skin. He raised his hand as she struggled upright.

"Easy, lady. Gather your strength. Marcus wishes to see you."

Jasirey evened out her breathing. "Who are you?"

"Mtombe. You . . . would not recall." Removing his zip-up jacket, he placed it around her shoulders and handed her a bottle of water.

Jasirey peered into kind, worried eyes. "I remember you from the Imperiatu. You wanted to leave the Devoted. To work for Marcus?"

"What? No. The first mate hired me. When I realized . . . I intended to disembark when we return to Africa. I have no papers for

America." His hands lifted, unconsciously pleading. "Lady, I am but one against many."

Jasirey gathered her wits. *Robin fell. Please let him be all right.* "Promise me you won't endanger yourself if you have no safe way to help."

Eyes lowered, Mtombe meant to shake his head but found himself nodding. He felt pulled to meet Jasirey's eyes, the color of a calm blue ocean. His racing pulse slowed.

She squeezed his hand. "I need a few minutes to prepare. Please." He bowed and stepped out.

Hard and warm to the touch, Jasirey's breasts throbbed. She had been unconscious for some time. She'd suffered clogged ducts once before while nursing Christopher—excruciatingly painful and, if left untreated, leading to infection and fever, even delirium.

Marcus likely had little knowledge of breast health, something Jasirey could use to thwart him, rob him of his toy, and preserve her sanity. She harbored no illusions that anything less was at stake.

Mtombe held off the impatient mercenaries with the excuse that their prisoner needed the toilet. When Jasirey stepped out, she remained steady on her feet but looked terribly pale. He placed a firm hand under her elbow and staked the claim to escort her. His hand trembled as they reached the entrance to Marcus's stateroom. Jasirey's fingers skimmed his with the briefest of touches, and his breathing steadied.

❧ ❧ ❧

Marcus offered Jasirey a glass of wine.

"I'd prefer tea if you have it," she said.

He gestured to a sideboard that held a coffeepot and an electric teapot.

"I'd suggest one cup." He smiled pleasantly. "Lessens bladder accidents."

No hint of a tremor rattled Jasirey's cup as she sat across a desk from Marcus. She realized his eyes were pale yellow. They registered appreciation. For the challenge she presented, she supposed. Softly heavy breasts, milk expressed, lay against her chest and reminded Jasirey her children needed their mother. She'd entertain Marcus—buy her husbands time to find her—to the last dregs of her strength.

165

"I understand you're a sex trafficker. I can't imagine I'd be of much value."

"Quite the contrary, it seems. I received an offer." He smiled at the slight widening of her eyes. "First, let's enjoy becoming acquainted." He unfurled those thick fingers. "Your hand."

Breathe. Jasirey lifted her hand. Marcus drew out the production of kissing and tucking it into his elbow.

❧ ❧ ❧

Mtombe tagged behind the mercenaries to a room lit by a single overhead florescent strip. His stomach clenched. They called the ten-by-ten-foot cubicle the breakroom. A metal table with restraints and a cart to the side gleamed under the light. Four men whispered and laughed together along the room's bare perimeter. A lone man wearing bright yellow pants fidgeted near the table. Mtombe dragged his eyes away from the implements displayed on the cart.

The mercenaries flicked unwelcoming looks at him but didn't question his presence.

He feared he would be useless against so many.

The door opened. Affecting a courtly entrance, Marcus gently disengaged Jasirey's hand, then shoved her into the table. "Remove the clothing." His words chipped out like ice.

Four sets of careless hands lifted and dropped her face down onto the table. Mtombe slid out his knife and bulled past a man who restrained Jasirey's ankle. He slashed the seams of her dress and underwear, so they could be torn away without hurting her. Mtombe gritted his teeth as Marcus lightly slapped Jasirey's naked buttocks.

The air charged, and the room shrank. Though not a muscle twitched, the mercenaries seemed to lean in for the show. Turning his attention away from the table, Mtombe covertly studied them to anticipate moves and countermoves. Too many. He waited. He ticked off seconds, minutes. How long? How long could he close his ears to the sounds at the table?

The four who had secured Jasirey lurched forward at Marcus's command to open the shackles.

Seeing the faint marks on her wrists and ankles, Mtombe knew she must have used great strength to resist struggling against the restraints.

166

The men flipped her and tethered her back down.

Mtombe prepared to move as the mercenaries stared at Jasirey. Slowly, their bodies relaxed. Even Marcus's face went slack, his eerie eyes peaceful.

But before Mtombe could decipher their strange behavior, Marcus's eyes bulged. Mtombe saw red-hot intent scorch away the peacefulness. Time had run out. On the balls of his feet, he stepped toward the table and rammed his fist into Marcus's nose. A side kick sent the heavier man flying into the door, which screeched—a louder sound than the trafficker's howl—as the hinges broke and it thudded onto the hallway floor, Marcus sprawled over the top of it. The crash broke through the mercenaries' stupor.

Mtombe stepped into their midst.

Grunts. The dull thwap of fists to the gut. Sharper whacks to the face. Curses, sweat, and the metallic tang of blood permeated the room. Others rushed in. At the edges of his mind, Mtombe accepted his death.

✤ ✤ ✤

Blood streaming from his broken nose, Marcus raised himself up on an elbow as Strafe sidled past several strangers infiltrating the breakroom, grabbed the boss's arm, and jerked him to his feet.

"We have to get out of here," Strafe hissed.

Marcus's raptor eyes blazed. "Call the guards to set up with their rifles above the ramp and cover the dock." He grabbed Strafe's shirt. "Alive. I want her alive. Kill anyone helping her."

While Strafe ran to do Marcus's bidding, he brooded. Marcus had not exactly broken his promise to Strafe that he would see the woman Jasirey again. He'd had Strafe set up the coffee maker and an electric teakettle in his stateroom while guards went to bring her to the boss. The times Strafe had observed Jasirey for Marcus, she always drank iced tea. Hot was the best he could offer.

Marcus had signaled Strafe's dismissal before she saw him. He needed to speak to her. She had stuck in his mind since he first met her at the Vermont resort where Marcus had assigned him to spy on Ian.

Too old for his taste, not even beautiful except when she smiled, a smile she never aimed at him. He wanted that smile, just one. So, he had preceded Marcus to the breakroom. He would maybe have a few seconds to speak to her before Marcus started the breaking process.

All courtly fake gentleman, Marcus had ushered her in and ordered her tied to the table. Strafe moved to her side. Their eyes met. He cringed as the light of recognition dulled to disappointment. Expecting her to plead for help, an uncomfortable reaction instead raked over him. *You're better than this.*

Her gaze focused on his yellow pants. Glad for that as Marcus began, Strafe forced his clenched hands to stay down until Marcus's hired thugs turned her. Eyes the color of spruce trees filled his field of vision and dove deeper into his mind. He not only saw but felt the soft cushion of grassy shore and the pleasant warmth of a sunny light blue sky. He relaxed to the scent of clover and wildflowers mixed with brine from the pleasantly cool sea spray. He felt cradled in peaceful ease, his only concern just to be.

His eyes scrunched in concentration. *No, just one more minute.* But the sky darkened, warmth faded, and the sea roared with turbulence. Marcus's red rage seared the room.

Strafe pushed past a mercenary, mouth gaping, still caught in an apparently shared vision he knew Jasirey had somehow placed in their minds. All Marcus's thugs looked glassy eyed.

With the noise of the door breaking, the mercenaries snapped out of their trance and turned on the crewman who had kicked Marcus hard enough to land him and the door onto the hallway floor. Strafe didn't recognize the crewman.

The fine hairs on Strafe's neck had prickled as a thin voice he knew no one else heard said, "Help him." He realized she meant the crewman but had ignored her as he helped Marcus up and gave the guards the boss's orders.

❧ ❧ ❧

Nikolai, nose wrinkled in a delicate sneer, had stepped onto the ship accompanied by Andwar and Chen, two bodyguards all Marcus allowed when he agreed that Nikolai, posing as Iurii, should come to the merchantman to finalize the supposed deal to sell Jasirey to Iurii. The three men stoically accepted a crude search of their persons.

They had been escorted to an office below deck where a male wail of pain had blown Nikolai's plan apart.

Heaped on top of a cabin door, Marcus had sprawled on the floor two-thirds down the passageway. The Protectors incapacitated their escort. Nikolai hurtled past the unconscious Marcus and froze in the doorway.

Jasirey lay unconscious. Translucent skin showcased thundercloud colors blooming over red welts on her arms, torso, and legs. Her throat—Nikolai set aside his fury, left her to Andwar's care, and turned to help Mtombe who held off four assailants on his own.

Almost too tired to see straight, Mtombe barely managed to pull his punch away from a fiercely grinning Nikolai, who then charged toward one of his attackers. And two feet away, Chen. *God be praised.*

An alarm sounded, and the last mercenary crumpled. Hands on his thighs, Mtombe bent forward to pull in careful breaths past bruised ribs. "The gangplank will be guarded," he warned.

"Are you sound?" Nikolai asked Mtombe, who nodded. "Good. Carry Jasirey."

Wrapped in Andwar's jacket, she lay unnaturally still.

Marcus had disappeared and presumably set off the alarm.

The group stayed together until they reached the deck. Nikolai ordered Mtombe, holding Jasirey, into a utility closet, then set off with Chen and Andwar to scope out a safe way off the ship.

Jasirey mewled, and Mtombe used his chin to pet her hair. "It's all right, loveling. We have you."

Her eyes fluttered and fixed on Mtombe's worried gaze. Her voice rasped from her abused throat. "I waited."

Mtombe pressed his lips to her forehead.

Footsteps sounded heading toward them. Mtombe gently set Jasirey on the floor and grasped a mop handle in a horizontal hold.

Nikolai whispered before opening the door. "We encountered only token resistance. They have congregated at the dock. Waiting for Jasirey, Chen thinks."

Mtombe agreed. "He is not finished with her. His pride is in play."

Taking her weight on his forearms while he continued to grasp the mop handle in front of her at an angle, Mtombe again carried Jasirey. A whining ping sent them to the deck. They heard a grunt and a toppling thud before Chen appeared out of the shadows to beckon the men forward. He set a circuitous route. They encountered no further obstacles until they neared the dock.

Louder and more frequent gunshots pinned the group to one spot. Chen and Nikolai slid through the shadows toward the source of the gunfire. Mtombe set Jasirey on the deck and crouched over her. He winced at each report of gunfire.

A light signaled as Andwar approached, clutching a seeping wound in his upper arm. "The gangplank is open to snipers positioned above the area."

Mtombe stewed in frustration. Jasirey struggled to sit up, and he said, "Stay down, loveling." She became agitated. He turned to enlist Andwar's help and whirled back as she gained her feet.

Her words ground out slowly but distinctly. "Stay behind me. Wants me alive."

❋ ❋ ❋

Strafe had a bad feeling. No way could Jasirey's people bypass the guns but—bad feeling. No marksman himself, he stood behind the sniper nearest the gangplank. He must speak to her. As to what he might say, thoughts spun like a hamster's wheel.

The sniper started to weave. His rifle dipped and hit the deck. Head lolling, the man slid down the bulkhead. Strafe checked the man for injuries but found none. He appeared to be sleeping peacefully.

Reaching for the gun, Strafe stilled, paralyzed with fear by the threat in the unfamiliar ice-blue eyes that bored into his. The man cable-tied Strafe's hands behind his back and handed him down the ladder to another man he didn't know.

Strafe watched Jasirey move toward them. More hurt than he'd realized, she nonetheless managed to soothe Marcus's three canine beasts into lying down. Their great heads rested on their outstretched paws. Slick as you please, Jasirey and her rescuers walked off the ship with Strafe as prisoner.

❋ ❋ ❋

Liu rendered first aid on the plane. He agreed with Mtombe's assessment that his ribs were merely bruised. Andwar and Jasirey required hospitalization, but Liu stabilized them for transport to Boston where Jesse would keep him apprised of their treatment.

170

Ian, Lee, and Fael questioned Mtombe. He lifted a heavy head. "I stood useless, listening to Marcus taunt her, 'Answer me,' though he never asked a question. He wished her to beg and promise to tell him anything."

"Which she did not do," Fael said.

Mtombe's fists clenched. "Marcus ordered her turned to face him. Something happened. His eyes became unfocused. Did I not know better, I would say peaceful until they were not. I do not know why, but he meant to kill her." Upright through the recital, Mtombe gave in to bone-deep weariness and slumped into his chair.

"Thank you," Liu said. "I understand you do not have the legal papers required to stay in America, but you shall be safe at the compound for a few days. Jasirey will wish to see you."

Mtombe nodded, though he hoped for some time to himself first. His conflicted thoughts looped continuously around unconsciously calling Jasirey loveling.

❧ ❧ ❧

In the hospital in Boston, Andwar heard that Jasirey ordered Fael, Lee, and Kimika to accompany the children home and barred everyone else from her room. A bullet had passed through Andwar's upper arm without hitting anything vital. He wheeled his IV pole down the corridor and into Jasirey's room. As he expected, she lay awake.

Andwar's dark eyes squarely met hers. "I'm sorry about your driver. I'm told he was a friend." He regretted his wound prevented him from holding Jasirey through the pain swamping her. He remained silent until she battled it down.

"Nikolai, Chen, and I have not yet reported the mission details to Lee and Fael."

Jasirey spoke haltingly through her abused throat. "You okay?"

Andwar refused to be sidetracked. "It is our duty—" Flashing eyes halted him.

"Is your loyalty to them or to me?"

"They're one and the same."

"Do you trust me?"

"Without reservation."

"My goals will not always mesh with my husbands' nor the Imperiat's when their priority is to keep me safe, especially when at the expense of someone else's safety."

Again, Andwar wished he could hold her as grief swept through her once more.

Jasirey attempted a weak smile. "No doubt following me will sometimes go against your first instincts as my Protectors."

Andwar could not argue with her assessment.

"Please wait on your report just for a little bit. I need time to think."

He bowed. "As you wish."

❧ ❧ ❧

After a broken and dislocated ankle, Jasirey had learned in her teens that she possessed a high tolerance for pain and the ability to focus past it. On Marcus's ship, she faced irrefutable proof of the gifts the Devoted had been hinting they saw in her.

After drinking tea in Marcus's stateroom, she had given him her hand. He ceremoniously tucked it around his arm and led her to a room where three chained dogs—a Rottweiler, a German Shepherd, and a larger Mastiff—came to attention.

"One gesture from me, and they would tear you limb from limb," he said.

At the satisfied tone in his voice, Jasirey made her first stupid move. He had no intention of feeding her to the dogs, at least not before he had a turn at her. She took a step forward. The dogs' ears flattened, and their low growls vibrated in her chest.

"Once given, a dog's loyalty is absolute," Marcus said. "They obey not out of fear or lust for material rewards. Their sole desire is to please the head of the pack, to gain his approval."

"Unlike people." Jasirey tugged gently until Marcus released her. She held out her hands to the dogs. They whined and cast furtive looks at Marcus. Jasirey whispered in calm tones. The dogs sniffed, nuzzled her fingers, and allowed her to scratch their ears. She saw a jar of dog biscuits and fished out three. The dogs gulped them down, then one after another dropped and rolled to their backs, bellies exposed.

Body rigid, Marcus stood as though in a thrall. Soon enough, he shook himself and courteously offered his arm to lead her to another room that seemed even smaller with leering men lining its walls. Marcus's demeanor hardened to pure malice.

Marcus usually used the breakroom simply for business—to train recalcitrant commodities—pirated human beings—or to obtain

172

information quickly. Marcus would enjoy bending Jasirey to his will. He would deal with the dogs later.

Jasirey concentrated on what lay deep within him. In her mind, his roiling thoughts translated to razor-sharp pitchforks goading him. The image eased her trembling.

Rough hands tethered Jasirey to the table, her arms overhead and her legs stretched to the corners. Gentler hands tore away her clothing. *Breathe. Oh, God, naked. Focus.*

Marcus lightly slapped her bottom. "Time for a discussion, highness."

Unable to see his eyes, her concentration wavered. A young man stepped into her line of vision. *Nice face, intelligent eyes. Why had he settled for this life? Wait.* He had hit on her at the pool in Vermont, the restaurant in Boston—he was Marcus's spy. *No help there.*

Something tracked down her bare back. Jasirey focused on the young man's bright yellow pants.

"I'll know if you lie," Marcus said softly. "You won't enjoy the consequences." Jasirey braced, and Marcus chuckled. "Who are the Devoted and where do they reside?"

Her throat worked. Nothing came out. The thing on her back lifted and cracked down on her butt. The sound startled her more than the sting and loosened her tongue. "An island, I've no idea where. Ian handles travel arrangements."

"One of those pampered women who expects to be taken care of, are you?"

A faster slash, this time on her shoulder blades. The yellow pants wavered through her watering eyes.

"I believe you, highness. Think what a lie will bring. What does 'Jasirey' mean?"

She breathed slowly, stared at Yellow Pants, couldn't remember the name the young man had given her. She drew out her answer. "It's the title of the person . . . chosen. The Devoted say destined. Destiny, reincarnation—it's hazy for me. I'm a figurehead. I don't lead . . . anything. Each generation passes on stories. Traditions accumulated over centuries. If the name ever had a meaning, they haven't mentioned it. They call me their lady."

And suddenly in her mind, flashing in purple neon—Revered Vessel. Jasirey meant revered vessel.

"You disappoint me, highness." The esses echoed and hissed. "An obvious and vain attempt to stall for time. Ah well, victory is often about the process, is it not?"

Too thin for a belt, knobby in texture, the object floated gently up her spine. Someone yanked Jasirey's hair. She smelled leather as it passed over her nose and mouth and looped about her neck.

"Tell me what I want to know." Marcus's silky voice invited, persuaded. The noose tightened fractionally on each word.

Jasirey's vision blurred. The tension released. The thing scraped across and away from her throat to bite into her back and legs. Another yank at her hair. An experienced singer, she silently filled her lungs.

"Answer me." Spots formed on the yellow pants. Blows, spots— Jasirey lost track of the rounds. She said nothing and sensed Marcus's escalating excitement.

"Now, highness," he said companionably, "let's begin again."

Uncaring fingers pried at the restraints digging into her, flipped her face up, and tightened them once more against her abraded skin. Her gaze wheeled about the room, seeking Marcus, needing to see his eyes.

He wanted her pleading submission but hoped for the defiance he could continue to thrash. She latched on to his pallid eyes, bored through ice deeper and deeper to the heaving lava core. The room faded. Energy, raw and palpable, bridged the gap between them.

Jasirey saw his will, sharp and hard as a peach pit, and eased hers through the runnels to lure him to rest. His face slackened, his mouth drooped. Those eerie eyes quieted. Jasirey felt her control waver, steady, weaken, and slip away—a second mistake that fully roused the cyclonic fury within Marcus.

The quirt—a riding whip—slashed. Spittle spewed from Marcus's lips. Jasirey writhed under the blows to her breasts. Mtombe came between them. And there her memory ended until she woke on the ship's deck.

Semi-conscious and in shock, she managed only disjointed images. Cold eyes sighted down cold steel barrels. No appeal of kindness or goodness moved them. Jasirey ordered. Down, sit down, sleep.

At the top of the gangplank, fangs bared, Marcus's three snarling dogs stood sentry to stop her and her men. Nikolai and Chen raised the rifles they'd confiscated.

"No." Jasirey's hand rose and slowly lowered. The dogs shifted, whined, and lay on the deck. Jasirey patted them. *Good dogs, good boys,* she projected at them and knew they understood.

She saw Andwar holding onto the young man wearing yellow pants with his good arm. She would later find out his name was Strafe. "Bring him with us," she said to Nikolai, who assumed she wanted the man in order to gain information from him on Marcus. Jasirey had a feeling—she would no longer dismiss her feelings—that the young man would be important.

No one harried her rescuers on their route to the plane.

Jasirey assumed the banished Ian and Liu and probably Mtombe haunted the hospital hall outside. Mtombe had called her "Loveling." Under pressure, true, but clear to her, he had gone way beyond prophecy to help her. Her wild boar. Weirdly, she harbored less ambivalence for Mtombe than for Nikolai, Andwar, Chen, Favian, and Sajan—she dubbed them the five—quite possibly because she had no intention of telling Mtombe he was the wild boar of her prophecy. He still needed to find his destined path.

Her stomach hurt, her breasts, and her throat. Worse, Jesse decreed she had to wean the babies to heal properly. Her hospital room phone rang. Expecting her sons to call and with no one to hear the ring and answer it for her, Jasirey allowed a small groan of pain as she reached for it.

"Hello, highness." Marcus waited a beat.

Jasirey said nothing. For the moment, he incited neither fear nor loathing. At his chuckle, she said, "You've nothing to gain from me, Marcus." His fight for composure bled through the line.

"You do intrigue me, highness." An intonation of warmth curled through his voice. "I look forward to our next encounter and to meeting your children." Still no response. He sighed. "I concede round one. I underestimated you." Ice crept into his tone. "I'd be fascinated to learn how you enticed my dogs to obey you. You won't find Strafe as biddable."

"Who knows? Your dogs would have gone with me of their own free will."

"You think so?"

She sensed a second of panic under the scoffing tone. Shrewdness replaced it.

"You're saying you can bring men to heel as easily as dogs."

Crap. Third mistake. Think strategically, she cautioned herself. Marcus didn't yet realize it, but she knew he craved the momentary peace she'd given him for the first time in his memory, a craving he might not be able to define but would seek with a vengeance and would eventually consider a weakness that must be destroyed.

"Dogs follow both the male and female alpha," she said.

Marcus's voice lightened. "So they do."

Finally, the right move. Marcus would not punish the dogs.

"It is rare for me to lose my temper." He hesitated. "No permanent damage, I trust?"

"Fate intervened."

"Ah, is that what it was? Interesting theory but don't downplay your ability to endure. I won't. I'll dig for details on the Devoted to prepare for Round 2. Sleep well, highness."

Like that would happen. The safety of the island lay far away. Revered vessel—the Imperiat considered her that in the sense of carrying and harboring her children. She believed it meant that, like a blood vessel, she transported something vital to the world. What exactly, she didn't yet know. One thing was clear. She no longer had the liberty to ignore what she sensed—foresight, for instance. She might have had a chance to stop Robin's murder if she had cultivated that gift.

Jasirey considered what-ifs useless and instead focused on the meaning of the colors that had haunted her since her vision in the Imperiatu. She'd gotten images from Marcus's men of Africa. Parched and withering grasslands, rivers clogged with orange mud or drying under the harsh yellow sun to blanched, cracked bumps and swells— desertification.

No red, however, as had also been in her vision. Sometimes considered the color of war—something she feared could happen over water rights—red could also stand for the heart, for love. Her gifts worked better with positive emotions.

Under normal circumstances, she would not be able to duplicate what she had accomplished on Marcus's ship. The trauma she suffered unleashed abilities she now believed possible but had no idea how to access at will or how to control.

Jasirey vowed to accept the training the Devoted offered. Whether at home or on the island, they would decide together. She would demand more of a partnership. Whatever knowledge the Devoted possessed, she needed. And to reciprocate, whatever she sensed, she would share no matter how unreal or bizarre.

One thing she accepted without doubt. Along with all the wonderful things in her new life—her husbands, children, the Devoted—trouble lay in wait, and she would do everything possible to be ready for it.

Acknowledgments

Thank you to

—Alex Arnot for his help from delivering books to fixing computer glitches

—to copy editor and editorial consultant Phillis Scott for her astute comments and suggestions

—to cover artist Elizabeth Lindgren for a second great cover

—to my publisher and editor Marcia Gagliardi for her insistence that muddy prose be made as clear as a mountain stream

Bonnie Arnot

About the Author

Bonnie Arnot loves stories about female heroes conquering new worlds as well as narratives about historical places and people who can seem just as fantastical to the modern world. She lives in western Massachusetts with her husband, two sons, and two cats.

Colophon

Text for *Husbands of Jasirey* is set in Baskerville, a serif typeface designed in 1757 by John Baskerville in Birmingham, England, and cut into metal by punchcutter John Handy. Baskerville is a transitional typeface intended as a refinement of old-style typefaces of the period, especially those of his most eminent contemporary, William Caslon.

Compared to earlier designs popular in Britain, Baskerville increased contrast between thick and thin strokes, making serifs sharper and more tapered. He also shifted the axis of rounded letters to a more vertical position. Curved strokes are more circular in shape and the characters more regular, creating a greater consistency in size and form influenced by the calligraphy Baskerville had learned and taught as a young man.

Baskerville's typefaces remain popular in book design.

Titles for *Husbands of Jasirey* are set in Brioso Pro, a new typeface family designed in the calligraphic tradition of the Latin alphabet. Brioso displays the look of a finely penned roman and italic script, retaining the immediacy of hand lettering while having the scope and functionality of a contemporary composition family. Brioso blends the humanity of written forms with the clarity of digital design, allowing designers to set pages of refined elegance. Designed by Robert Slimbach, this energetic type family is modeled on his formal roman and italic script. In the modern calligrapher's repertoire of lettering styles, roman script is the hand that most closely mirrors the oldstyle types that we commonly use today; it is also among the most challenging styles to master. Named after the Italian word for lively, Brioso moves rhythmically across the page with an energy that is tempered by an ordered structure and lucidity of form.